My eyes foc the immediate m...... against mine made me very conscious of how close she was sitting to me.

I sighed and pushed down a sudden urge to pin her to the futon. I moved away and she moved closer again.

"Does alcohol always have this effect on you?" I asked.

"Yes. No."

I narrowed my eyes at her.

"I've only had one drink. And a bit. Although…I do feel a bit funny," she confessed.

"You said Billy gave you acetaminophen?"

"I thought it was."

She reached down to the floor, and her T-shirt slid up, exposing the smooth skin on the small of her back. I ached to lean over and run my fingers along it. I had to grip my knees tightly to stop myself from doing it. She handed me an unmarked, white pill bottle and I grimaced as I opened it.

"These aren't just acetaminophen," I informed her. "These are prescription. With codeine."

Her arm was still draped across my lap, and I tried unsuccessfully to disentangle myself from her. She sighed and buried her head against my chest. I could smell my shampoo in her hair, and knowing she'd used it did nothing to ease my increasingly apparent desire.

She turned her face toward me, and I found myself staring into her slate-coloured eyes. Her pupils were big, her skin was pink, and when she parted her lips to speak again, I had to look away in order to control myself.

Tattoos
and
Tangles

by

Melinda Anne Di Lorenzo

This is a work of fiction. Names, characters, places, and incidents are either the product of the author's imagination or are used fictitiously, and any resemblance to actual persons living or dead, business establishments, events, or locales, is entirely coincidental.

Tattoos and Tangles

COPYRIGHT © 2013 by Melinda Anne Di Lorenzo

All rights reserved. No part of this book may be used or reproduced in any manner whatsoever without written permission of the author or The Wild Rose Press, Inc. except in the case of brief quotations embodied in critical articles or reviews.
Contact Information: info@thewildrosepress.com

Cover Art by *Debbie Taylor*

The Wild Rose Press, Inc.
PO Box 708
Adams Basin, NY 14410-0708
Visit us at www.thewildrosepress.com

Publishing History
First Crimson Rose Edition, 2013
Print ISBN 978-1-62830-079-6
Digital ISBN 978-1-62830-062-8

Published in the United States of America

Dedication

To my family.
You make every day a little bit more of my own HEA.

Acknowledgments

Eternal thanks to Dj Hendrickson for being a fun, patient editor, and to my beautiful cheerleading squad—Shelley B, Margarita R, and Sharon R.

Chapter One

A tattoo parlour has a distinctive smell. Anyone who tells you otherwise is a liar, or hasn't been inside one. The exact source of the scent is elusive, though. It smells like sweat, and heat, and something else that's altogether intangible. It's like too many bodies mingling with ink and blood and ammonia.

Yun's was no different.

When we walked in—Blair and I—it fairly reeked of all that. And some of the nervous sweat was pouring off my own body, mingling in the air with countless others.

An Asian man with a bald head was sitting behind the glass countertop display case, and he glanced up and grinned cockily at Blair. I wondered if he was Yun, in the flesh.

"Let me guess," he said in English with just the barest hint of an accent. "A colourful butterfly on the small of your back. Or the Chinese symbol for *HOPE*, accompanied by a tiny dragon. Right above your bellybutton."

Blair rolled her eyes.

"For one," she told him from underneath her bejewelled ball cap, "you're Korean. I wouldn't ask a Korean man for a Chinese tattoo. He'd fuck it up even more than a white guy would."

She turned around and bent over, exposing the

smooth, tanned skin of her lower back to the tattoo artist. She was showing off her body just as much as she was showing of the *un*-tattooed state of her skin. That was just her way.

I saw his eyes widen in surprise and glitter with appreciation.

Blair is a good example of the female form, there's no denying it. She's all curves and softness and ridiculously lush brown hair.

"For two," my friend added as she spun back around, "I'm a virgin."

She was talking about tattoos, and the Korean guy must've known it too, but his jaw dropped a little anyway.

"We both are," Blair said.

She made a sweeping gesture to include me in her description. The tattoo artist turned to me as if just noticing I was there.

I smiled wryly to myself.

I blend. It's true.

Part of it is because subtle is who I am. I favour the colours brown, dark green, and tan.

Mocha, forest, and sandstorm, Blair always corrects in a teasing voice as she tries to entice me with red—*fire*—or purple—*plum*—or even pink—*blush*.

My eyes are almost gray, though my driver's license claims they're blue. My hair is fine, and wavy, and nothing but blonde. I don't wear makeup because I've never met a kind that doesn't make me sweat, and I can't do highlights because every chemical makes me break out in hives. I was predesigned to fit into a crowd.

But part of my wallflower-esque appearance is also

by design.

I don't want to draw any attention to myself, so I choose to keep quiet. I try to maintain an introspective attitude. I picked a career working with deaf kids so I can get away with not being noisy, and no one minds. I am deliberately careful in everything I do.

Think now. Act later. Or act never. *Always.*

Every time I've gone around that little mantra, bad things have happened.

Case in point, Dean. I winced, and pushed down the image of his face as it threatened to rise to the surface.

I preferred to leave the standing out to Blair. She's good at it, she likes it, and it takes the pressure off me. The evidence was in the way Yun was staring at her now.

I cleared my throat and when he turned to look at me, I tried to smile. I failed, and he went back to ogling my friend. I sighed internally and waited it out. I wasn't in a hurry. After all, the tattoo wasn't a spontaneous decision. It was a part of my carefully laid out plan to move past the sadness. It served a dual purpose—to help me move forward, and to honour the memory of my sister.

"Virgins, huh?" Yun made the word sound dirty.

Blair grinned and he winked at her. She had him wrapped around her little finger with just a few sentences and a look at her ass.

"I'm Ji-Hun," he said. "I can help you out with that little problem."

"For a good price?" Blair asked.

"Of course," Ji-Hun Yun agreed quickly without asking what we needed.

"Cass wants something pretty specific," my friend told him.

"Does she?" He didn't bother to hide his disappointment that it was me, and not Blair, he'd be de-virginizing. "Boyfriend's name in a heart? Picture of puppy?"

"Not exactly," Blair replied, and motioned at me to show him my drawing.

I handed it to Ji-Hun silently. I saw his eyes flicker with interest as he looked first at me, then the paper.

"Where'd you get this?" he asked.

"I drew it," I said.

He looked like he wanted to argue that, and I prepared to defend myself. But Blair leaned across the counter, exposing the better part of her chest to the man, and whispered in his ear. I couldn't hear what she said, but I held my breath until Ji-Hun nodded. He handed me a clipboard.

"Answer the questions," he instructed. "Make sure you're being honest, or my ass is on the line. When you're done, sign it to say you've understood it all perfectly."

I read through the waiver quickly.

Was I over 18 and of sound mind/not under the influence? Yes.

Did I have any conditions which would impair healing? No.

Did I release the artists from liability? Yes.

I answered them without pausing until I got to the very last one.

Did I have the rights to the original artwork?

I carefully weighed the question in my mind. The drawing was mine. The place I had copied it from…I pushed that image down quicker than I had pushed down the memory of Dean's face. I was suddenly doubtful.

"You okay?" Blair asked.

I nodded.

"You thinking about Jeanette?"

I nodded again.

"There's still time to get a puppy," Ji-Hun interrupted, and Blair glared at him.

"This is the least sensible thing I've ever done," I whispered to my friend. "What if every time I look in the mirror, I see the way it looked...on her?"

My friend shrugged. "You have a logic I don't understand, Cass. When you decided to do this, I was surprised. But I'm proud of you. It's commemorative. It's defiant. It's a slap in the face of the bad things that've happened to you."

"It is?" I said, even though she was quoting my own argument back to me.

"And it's not the least sensible thing you've done," she told me.

"No?"

Blair smiled. "No way. Marrying Dean takes the cake on any tattoo you'll ever get."

I grinned as I ticked *YES*. Only Blair could make me laugh about him.

Yun sighed as I handed him the form. Was he disappointed? Did he expect me to balk at the questions, then change my mind? But he just met my eyes and unwrapped a new pair of gloves from a sealed box.

"Don't worry if you're allergic to latex," he said with a sly glance at Blair. "The only things I keep in here made of *that* stuff have a completely different purpose."

My friend ignored his innuendo and smiled encouragingly at me.

"This is it," she told me. "Say goodbye to the past and hello to the future!"

I wasn't sure whether or not it was ironic that I was doing something permanent to my body to erase the scars in my heart and mind. It was something I had to do. I had been living with the deep ache for too long.

I took a big breath and hopped up into the chair. I had to straddle it so my shoulder would be properly exposed, and I shifted awkwardly, trying to get comfortable. I felt mildly debaucherous as I settled in. I was in a tattoo parlour. My short legs were spread in a very unladylike way around the sides of the chair. The plastic creaked under me, and Blair giggled. She grabbed my sweater and yanked it off. I looked at it in her lap. It was reassuringly modest, and a soothing shade of brown.

"Mocha," Blair whispered as if she could hear my thoughts.

Yun moved around the room quickly and efficiently. He was muttering to himself in Korean, and after a few minutes, his plastic, non-latex gloves pressed something onto my back. Whatever it was had the texture of wax paper, and crinkled quietly like it, too. It was unnerving. He pushed a wet cloth against the paper, and I almost giggled as I imagined one of those kids' transferable tattoos of a giant smiley face appearing on my shoulder.

My humour was short lived, though.

A noisy buzz reverberated through the room, and

continued down across my shoulders as Yun touched the needle to my skin. I bit my lip to keep from whimpering. I'm not good with pain, and the pinch was close to excruciating.

"Is it awesome?" Blair asked.

"Why don't you try it and find out?" I replied through gritted teeth.

"No, thanks," she said breezily. "My employer frowns upon body modifications."

"You're a waitress," I reminded her.

"Hostess," she corrected. "And it's the only place where I can keep it classy."

"That woman in the kitchen has tattoos up and down both her arms!" I protested. "And she's got at least one piercing I've seen."

"That's a man." Blair popped a piece of gum into her mouth and gave it a deliberately obnoxious snap.

I made a face even though I wasn't sure she could see it. "No, the lady. With the rose up one side and a dragon up the other."

"Yes. That's Doug."

"Doug…ette?"

Blair laughed. "Trust me, he's a dude."

"Are you sure?" I asked.

"Oh, yes," my friend assured me. "I'm very sure."

I didn't push it. I didn't want to know how she knew. I didn't even want to think about it.

"Arg," I said as Yun hit a sensitive spot.

"Easy," the Korean man muttered.

"It hurts," I stated needlessly.

"It's supposed to," Yun replied. "And it's supposed to be a good pain. Like a loose tooth. You're gonna want more."

I wanted to argue with that statement as the needle made its way across my back without mercy. Why would anyone want more? I didn't even want to carry on with *this* one. But I had committed, and I had done it for a reason.

A chair slid across the floor, and then Blair's hand was in mine, squeezing it tightly.

I resisted the nearly overwhelming urge to close my eyes against the pain. It would feel too much like giving in. And each time I had closed them over the last few years—to sleep, to think, to breathe without having to look at the world—the faces of my past stung me worse than the tattoo gun. The exhaustion of keeping my eyes open was wearing on me, and I was already starting to look older than I was. I'd begun to feel like I was drowning.

I glanced up at the skull-shaped clock on the wall, and made an unintentional calculation.

It had been nearly two years since I had kicked Dean out. Six hundred and fifty-nine days. Each day I got up and reminded myself that I was better off without him—even on the loneliest mornings. Today was the official first anniversary of being completely unattached. But that wasn't the problem, or the source of most of my sadness, and my incredible fight to move on.

My true problem was that counting Days-Without-Dean reminded me of exactly how long it had been since I had seen Jeanette. Two thousand, nine hundred days since I had last seen *her* alive. I counted them the way an addict counts sober days. And still her image haunted me. It did more than that. It pained me. It tormented me. It made my heart want to stop beating.

I tried hard to steer my thoughts clear of her, but as I did, I went automatically back to Dean. It was an emotional ping-pong battle. Don't think of Jeannette. Think of Dean. Don't think of Dean. Think of Jeannette. The only way their lives had ever crossed was in the form of my memories. Their faces always mingled there, tightly wrapped together because of my emotions.

I remembered meeting Dean. Jeannette hadn't been gone long then, and I'd been struggling to remain in the world of the living. I'd had my eyes closed, and I'd been letting her face swim in the front of my mind.

"Hey," said a soft voice in my ear.

I ignored it because it cut through where I wanted to be—in the past.

"You think you could help me?" the voice persisted.

I'd opened my eyes then, and met the pained stare of one of the former group-home kids who'd been sucked along to the paintball course to supervise those of us still stuck in the system.

"I twisted my ankle," he told me. "I was going to go upstairs to get some ice, but the elevator's busted."

I'd helped him up reluctantly. When we reached the top of the stairs, I turned to go and he stopped me.

"Why aren't you out there?" he asked.

I snorted. "I'm not the paintball type."

"What type *are* you?" he'd wanted to know.

I looked up at him. He was tall, and not too good-looking in a way boys my age just couldn't manage. He carried his height without awkwardness, his stubble was real, and he *needed* me. At least at that moment. And it was the first time anyone had asked me a personal question that had nothing to do with Jeannette in what felt like a very long time. So I had paused to answer him.

"What's to like about it?"

"It's exhilarating. It makes me feel powerful. And I like to win," he said.

His face was intense and sincere, and it drew me to him.

"I'm Dean," he'd said.

"Cass."

"So…no paintball?"

I shook my head vehemently.

"I'll take you another time, and show you how good it can be," he offered.

"No, thanks."

But it was too late. I was already sucked into his world, misled by his charm.

And that night he had kissed me for the first time. Carefully. Like he was testing the waters even more cautiously than I would have. I hadn't *not* kissed him back, but I hadn't jumped in with both feet, either.

"I like you," he announced, sounding shy.

"I like you, too," I replied, feeling a bit surprised at the admission.

He kissed me again, and the second time, I kissed him back, too.

It was endearing. It was simple. And it was the beginning of a time in my life I would never get back.

"Cass?" Blair said softly, bringing me back to the present.

I focused on her voice and dragged myself out of my reverie.

"Yeah?" I murmured.

"Stop it."

"Okay," I agreed.

She knew about my problem. Or problems. That's what best friends are for.

The buzzing on my back finally stopped, and I heard Ji-Hun Yun stand up.

"Stay there a minute," he commanded.

He came back a moment later and started taping something sticky over my fresh ink.

"Plastic wrap," he explained. "And Vaseline."

Blair snorted. "No shit."

"No shit," Yun replied with a smirk in his voice. "Don't shower. Don't take it off. Nothing wet or…rubby…for forty-eight hours. Got it?"

"Got it," Blair answered for me, then she grabbed my hand gleefully. "Now let's go get drunk!"

Chapter Two

At first I almost ignored the girls as they came sauntering out of the tattoo place. They were giggling to themselves and didn't even see me tucked into the archway beside the shop. That made me roll my eyes a bit. I kind of wanted to grab them and shake them both and ask them if they had any idea who could be lurking around in a neighbourhood like that one.

I laughed at myself.

Because it wasn't really a bad part of town at all. And I was the one lurking.

I watched them stop for a second, and the taller, plumper one grabbed the shorter, thinner one by the shoulders. I paused. There was something endearing about the little blonde one. She smiled up at her friend, who whispered something I couldn't hear, then tugged the shorter one's sweater.

What did they have done? Was it both of them? Or just one getting a tattoo, and the other was there for her support?

I eyed the brunette. If it was only one of them, it was probably her. She looked like the type to get something typical and cutesy—a flower or a dragonfly, maybe. But I was curious anyway. I peered through the darkness to see if I could get a look at evidence of fresh ink on her back. I'm a sucker for tattoos. My own body is proof of that.

It was far too hard to see, though, and when I stepped forward to try to get a better look, I stumbled ever-so-slightly before pulling myself together.

Dammit, I cursed, and then added, *Damn yourself, Seever, for drinking those shots of whiskey before leaving the house.*

But I had been so frustrated lately, and it had seemed like an easy way to dull my senses.

"And dulled they are," I muttered under my breath.

The voluptuous brunette glanced up as if she heard me, and I stepped back into the shadows. She paused for just a second and grabbed her friend by the hand and yanked her along, laughing again.

I glanced at the glowing sign above Yun's and willed myself to go in—and to make this be the right one. My contacts had left me a sudden tip that led me right to this very shop, but it wasn't the most convenient of times. I was three drinks in, and cranky. I was definitely too drunk to take bad information with any kind of grace. This was the sixth tattoo place I'd tried in as many months. I'd been doing my best to keep any attention regarding this little pursuit of mine to a minimum. It's much harder to keep a low profile with an entourage, so I was alone, as usual. And that meant I hadn't brought anybody along to keep me in check.

I was truly torn for a moment.

I watched the two women as they disappeared around the corner, and I sighed. The shop was empty and it was near to closing time. I trusted my gut and ignored my conscience—which were *not* on the same page—and I went into the tattoo parlour.

"You Ji-Hun Yun?" I asked.

The Asian man behind the counter tensed when he

caught sight of me, and I smiled.

"Don't worry," I said in my quietest voice, "I have that effect on a lot of men."

Yun quivered and it made my smile widen even more. He was considering making a run for it. I'd seen the chicken shit expression on enough men's faces to recognize it.

"I'm fast," I told him casually. "I run ten miles a day, and I don't break a sweat. I'm strong, too. Probably bench what you weigh. How much is that? Hundred and thirty? Hundred and forty if you've had a couple burgers and shakes during the week?"

I could tell from Yun's face that he knew I wasn't telling him to brag. Sometimes it pays to be big. And sometimes it pays even more to point it out.

"This is actually my uncle's shop," he informed me in a heavy Korean accent. "I just do the work."

I didn't know if it was a lie, and I didn't care. But I did know that he'd been in Canada for thirty of his thirty-eight years. It was true that having a few drinks dulled my senses, but it didn't drown them out completely. I had still done my homework.

"Drop the phoney accent," I suggested. "And we'll talk."

"What do you want?" he replied, sullen but still nervous, and in near perfect English.

"I just have a couple questions about some ink. Think you could help me out?" I asked nicely.

Yun nodded once, and I pulled the photocopy out of my jeans pocket.

"I'm looking for some info on this," I explained as I handed it to him. "Maybe you've done it more than one time."

"No. I haven't."

I saw recognition pass across the Asian man's face, but it dissolved quickly back into guarded tension.

"You sure?" I asked, still in my nice-guy voice. "It would have been on a few girls who were on the unwilling side."

"You a cop?" he asked.

"Do I look like a cop?" I replied.

I didn't bother to feign offence. It was a valid question in our little exchange.

He did a once-over, and I let him check me out. Yes, my hair was military short, but that was about as close to cop as I came. My clothes were too expensive to be bought on a city salary. And my demeanour was just a little bit too cocky to belong to any kind of law enforcement personnel. He would see it in my eyes. I was nothing more than a mildly intoxicated, not-so-common criminal with a personal agenda. He met my gaze and I raised an eyebrow.

"So. Do you have an idea of how to lend me a hand?" I wanted to know.

Yun sighed at last. "Yeah."

"Good." My whole body was practically lit up with the excitement that one word brought. "Tell me."

"Well, aside from..." he trailed off.

"Aside from what?" I pushed.

Yun shook his head as if to clear it.

"Nothing. Just..."

"I'm not a patient man, Yun."

I put my fingers on his counter, and he watched as I tapped them slowly.

"Look," he told me nervously, "A guy called the shop—it was a seriously long time ago, I mean I want to say *years*—and was looking for someone to do some art off the books on some girl who might be…"

"Less than willing," I filled in, and Yun nodded.

"It was weird because people don't *call* for tattoos. Especially those kinds of tattoos. He also mentioned the specifics of the ink, something that sounded a little like that drawing. I don't know if it's the same one or not. But I said no. *We* run a legitimate place."

"*You* do?" I replied, picking up on his deliberate emphasis.

"Yes."

"But?"

"But I of know someone who still does that kind of stuff, no questions asked," he admitted.

"And you'll tell me who that is?" I tapped my fingers loudly on the counter.

He didn't answer me.

"For a fee," I added.

I watched Yun mentally weigh his options. He wasn't a dummy, and he was probably taking a risk by telling me anything. I'm good at reading people, and it was easy for me to make an assessment of the other man's price.

If his uncle was truly running a straight shop, he was paying taxes, paying rent, and keeping his tools serviceable. He probably had some walk-in clientele, as well as referrals and repeat customers. But he was also likely missing out on the seedier types. The ones who didn't want their art traceable through transaction records.

The ones like me. I smiled a small smile.

And if Yun really wasn't running the shop himself, he wasn't being paid top dollar by his uncle, either.

Watching his face, I pulled five hundred-dollar bills out of my wallet. It was enough to make him blink, but not so much that I looked desperate. I'd bet my left leg he didn't make that much on a good day. I put the money on the counter and Yun placed his hand on top of it.

"All right," he said a tad eagerly. "It's just a connection through a buddy's buddy."

I smiled again. I would've paid him ten times that amount if I thought his information would lead me in the right direction.

"Good enough," I replied mildly. "That's how I found *you*."

"Can I ask you where you got that picture?" Yun asked.

I started to tell him that no, he couldn't, but I changed my mind. I was feeling almost giddy with the knowledge that I was finally getting somewhere. I took my flask out of my pocket and took a celebratory swig. The whiskey was fuelling my enthusiasm.

"You give me the phone number of your buddy's buddy, and I'll tell you," I offered.

He pulled out an old fashioned Rolodex and flipped through until he found a card. As he handed it to me, I leaned closer to him, and let my smile become a grin.

"I pried it out my brother's cold, dead hands."

Chapter Three

The club was loud, and it smelled as bad as the tattoo parlour. Worse, even. It was crowded, too, and as I watched Blair gyrate on the floor, I wished for my comfy bed. Then I leaned against the cushioned booth bench and winced. My ink stung badly. It was going to be a while before anything was comfy again.

My friend moved effortlessly with the music, and I felt a small pang of envy. I was rarely jealous of her ease in a crowd or her ability with people. Blair was just Blair, and I appreciated her for who she was. But every now and then I wished I could join her in some of her antics. Maybe it would turn out to be exciting rather than terrifying.

But probably not, I admitted to myself as I watched her slide smoothly away from the unwanted attention of a particularly amorous stranger.

The song ended, and I could tell from the pouty face she made that the next one wasn't one she cared for. She came back to the table and signalled to a server I couldn't see. Moments later, drinks, shots and mixed, arrived in front of us. The server waved off my friend's attempt to pay. I shook my head. Only Blair.

"Drink up!" she shouted above the noise.

I couldn't be bothered to argue. I would've lost anyway. I shot back one of the two pink drinks with a grimace, then took a hefty sip of the clear one. My head was already buzzing like the tattoo gun.

"Right?" shouted Blair.

I stared at her, trying to make her face hold still.

"Right," I agreed half-heartedly.

I know some people drink to forget about their problems, and maybe it works for them. For me, though, it just makes it harder. When I'm drunk, I'm not in control, and when I'm not in control my mind wanders. But if I told Blair, she was going to tell me I was making excuses.

I took another sip and as I looked around the club, I remembered that one of the last times I saw Jeanette was in place like this. She'd been drinking heavily, as she often did in the last months of her life, and she kept pulling me onto the dance floor. I was fifteen, had no ID, and just wanted to go home. Then a bouncer had intervened, tossing us both out. Jeanette was angry at me for ruining her night.

I didn't understand it then, but her wild behaviour should've clued me in. I sighed so hard that the napkin under my drink fluttered..

"Hey!" Blair shouted. "Earth to Cass!"

Two more shots arrived. They were blue instead of pink, but I gulped one back at my friend's nod. Blair slid along the bench until she was practically in my lap. She still had to raise her voice to be heard, though.

"Feeling good?" she yelled, trying to be heard above the noise.

"No," I said emphatically.

"Dance?" she asked, ignoring my reply.

"S'kay," I answered with a head shake that made the room go wobbly. "Brain's already dancing."

"You can't sit here all sulky all night," Blair told

me.

"I'm not sulking," I sighed. "But I think I might be a bit tipsy."

"Hopefully more than a bit," my friend teased.

"This might've been a bad idea. I think I'm too old for this," I said.

Blair gave me a calculatedly dirty look. "If *you* are old, then *I* am old. And *I* am not old."

"Blair…"

"*We* are in our prime," she stated. "*We* are *twenty-three* years old. We are in our *prime,* I tell you!"

I could tell by her repeated emphasis that she wasn't going to give up. But I'm not a dancer, even when dancing is what everyone else is doing. The movements are complicated and I feel self-conscious and on display when I'm doing it.

"C'mon," I pleaded

"C'mon!" she said back in a firm voice.

Blair grabbed my hand and yanked me out onto the floor.

At least the club was so packed that it was hard to see where anyone was looking, and therefore easy enough to pretend they weren't watching me and my awkward moves.

Maybe this is my night. I gave my hips a little wiggle.

I didn't really feel like me, anyway. I'd left my mocha-coloured sweater at the table, and I was clad in a black (*midnight*) sleeveless top with a sequined back and a lacy front. It was Blair's own creation. She told me she'd pieced it together from three old shirts, but when she was done, it turned out to be too small for her.

"It's perfect for you," my friend had said with a

dangerous glint in her eyes.

I'd put it on, of course, and then she hadn't wanted me to take it off. It covered my freshly tattooed back, but left little to the imagination in the front. I was wearing her jeans, too, because she'd said no one could get a tattoo in khakis.

I lifted my arms and shimmied with my eyes closed, just this once grateful for my friend and her wicked ways. She put her hands on my shoulders and I giggled as I did an inappropriate rump shake against her hips. It was nice to have her to take care of me in my ongoing broken-hearted state. I was glad she hadn't just given up on me. I owed it to her to have a good time.

"I love you!" I shouted, trying to be heard over the thumping beat.

Blair didn't answer.

"I love you!" I yelled louder.

"Chill. It's only a dance, baby," growled a thick, male voice in my ear.

My eyes flew open and I realized it wasn't Blair behind me at all, but a greasy man in a damp, silk shirt. I tried to pull my arm out of his wiry grip, but he held on tight. I gave him a little shove. Someone—one of his friends, I assumed—laughed, and his hold loosened slightly as he turned to mouth off. I wriggled free. He wasn't much taller than I was, but his shoulders were twice as wide, and I could see a throbbing vein in his neck. He looked mean. And angry. His hostile expression frightened me a little, and I shrank away uncomfortably from his glare.

"Blair!" I called.

I looked around, feeling frantic and more than little drunk. The crowd was full of girls who could be her.

Tight jeans and spaghetti strap tanks were the wardrobe choice of the evening.

"Blair!"

There wasn't a lot of sense in shouting her name, but with my heart thumping the way it was, I couldn't think straight. The muscly little man grabbed my arm again, and I tried to shake him off.

"Chill," he said again and laughed. "My name's Monato. But you can keep calling me Blair if it makes things easier for you. How about I take you somewhere and give you something so you can relax?"

He was smiling, but he still had the angry look in his eyes and I saw that his friends were watching again, too. I looked down at my feet, wondering if the borrowed boots I was wearing had too much of a heel to make run for it.

Why did I let Blair talk me out of wearing my comfy flats?

"Hi, sweetheart."

I looked up and frowned. A pair of big brown eyes were gleaming down at me with concern.

"I was wondering where you were," the stranger told me.

"Me?" I squeaked.

"Of course, you," he replied.

"I'm…here," I said.

My head only reached his armpit, but his stance was nonthreatening. And he was more than big enough to fend off the 'roid monkey named Monato. The shorter man had already released my arm.

"Didn't realize she was *yours*," he muttered.

"She is," the brown-eyed man stated coolly.

"Since when?" Monato asked sullenly.

"Since now."

"All right." But Monato didn't back off quite yet.

The tall man slipped his fingers through mine and drew my hand up to his lips. He kissed each of my knuckles slowly while maintaining eye contact with Monato. Then he took my arm and wrapped it around his own waist before draping himself across my shoulders possessively. I was too startled to pull away.

"You need something else from me?" he asked.

I wasn't sure if he was talking to me or Monato, and I didn't trust myself to speak anyway. My hand was resting just above the dark-eyed stranger's waistband, and I could feel the shape of his well-muscled back through his thin dress shirt. He squeezed me a little bit tighter, and as my hand slipped down, it brushed something cold and hard.

A gun.

My mouth went dry and I willed myself not to gasp.

Don't be silly. How would he get a gun in here? Why would he have one?

But even as I moved my hand away from the metallic feel of whatever it was, I knew it couldn't be anything else.

Monato glanced back at his friends. They were all looking away nervously. I closed my eyes and said a little prayer he was just going to walk away. When I opened them again, he was gone, and I breathed a huge sigh of relief.

"Thank you," I said to the guy with the gun.

The gun!

I disentangled myself quickly hoping he wouldn't notice I'd felt it there in his waistband.

He assessed me with the same cool look he'd given Monato.

"Stay away from that guy," he warned, and strode away.

I had to force my mouth closed. I just about jumped out of my skin when a sweaty hand landed on my bare upper arm.

"Sorry, Cass. Did I scare you?" Blair asked with a grin.

"Yes. No."

"Well, which is it?" she teased.

"I don't know," I replied and then burst into tears.

"Hey! I'm sorry," my friend said. "I didn't mean to abandon you. Are you okay? What happened?"

I sobbed for a second more, trying to get hold of myself. When I was done, I realized Blair was looking at me expectantly. I hesitated. We share everything, but for some reason I didn't want to tell her about Monato or the man with the gun.

"It's been a long time, Cass," my friend said slowly. "We should be able to go out without…this."

She so rarely came down on me for my inability to heal. I felt terrible.

"It's not that," I told her, and realized it was pretty close to true. "I'm drunk. And I'm tired. And I hate men."

"That sounds so normal," she informed me with relieved smile.

"Thank you. I think."

"So you don't want one of these?" Blair held a martini glass up.

I took it and downed the drink. Whatever was in it made my throat burn. I hiccoughed and my friend giggled.

"We can go home," she told me.

"No. I just have to pee," I said.

"Do you want me to come?" she offered.

I shook my head. "I'll meet you back here in five."

I squished through the crowd, trying to make my way toward the flashing pink sign that indicated the location of the restroom. People pressed in on all sides, and for a few panicked seconds, I actually thought I wasn't going to be able to get there. But I finally reached the edge of the dance floor, and the crowd thinned. I breathed out.

My twenty seconds of inhibition were so *not worth this*.

I pushed on the swinging door, but it didn't budge. I pushed harder, but it still didn't move. I squinted in the dark, trying to see if it was a pull instead of a push, but there was no handle.

"What the hell?" I muttered.

I glanced at the men's room door. I looked around. It was unlikely it was going to be empty, but I told Blair the truth. I really had to go. And it was becoming urgent. I pushed on the door cautiously and it swung open. It smelled much worse than the ladies room, and I wrinkled my nose in disgust. I danced back and forth for one moment before I decided to just take a chance and make a run for it. With my head down, I raced for a stall. I locked myself in with a sigh. I went as quickly as I could, then peeked out before exiting. I couldn't see anyone inside so I once more bolted for the door.

"Never again," I muttered.

I saw them then, but it was too late.

Monato was holding the door while his buddies

blocked the way to the dance floor.

"Ladies room out of commission?" he asked.

"Door's stuck," was all I managed to stammer out.

Monato reached over and pushed. It swung open easily.

"It's not a coincidence," he told me with a smirk.

He took a short step toward me, and I frowned in puzzlement as his hands came up.

What's the towel for?

But before I could ask, it was around my face, covering my nose, and I could smell something acrid and gasoline-like that reminded me of a high school chemistry lab. I tried to pull the towel away, but someone held my hands against my sides. I shook my head violently and immediately realized my mistake. My struggle increased my need to get some air. Without meaning to, I gulped in the noxious fumes, and the room tilted around me. I had a roller coaster moment, as if my body was spinning and righting itself and then spinning again. I tried to control my inhales, to slow down my decent, but my senses were floaty, and confused, and I was hyperaware of the need to breathe. I gave in, and all the fight went out of my body as I lost consciousness.

Chapter Four

"What're you doing here?" said the kid behind the counter.

I growled at him for staring at me with his wide eyes and for his overly surprised tone. True, I didn't spend a lot of weekdays supervising the club, but that shouldn't have been enough to make him question my motivation.

"Are you my keeper, now?" I demanded.

"N-n-no," he stuttered, and I sighed loudly.

It was a kid I only vaguely recognized. Who the hell hired someone so young? He was probably barely old enough to be in there himself. I was now officially drunk, and not in the mood for new people.

"What're *you* doing here?" I asked, turning the question on him.

"I check coats," he replied.

"But you recognize me?" I wanted to know, and he nodded. "And you've probably heard the stories."

"S-s-some."

I sighed again, and wondered if he really had a stutter, or if he was just actually that nervous. I had heard some of the more exaggerated tales myself, and I didn't blame him for quavering a bit, but good God.

"Grow a set," I muttered.

"Pardon?"

"They're mostly made up," I confided. "I've never

killed a man for questioning me. If the question was a good one. And I'm probably not going to fire you for that look on your face."

"Okay," said the kid.

He looked only mildly relieved, and I found myself wondering if he'd be likely to wet his pants if I drew my gun and put it on the counter in front of him.

"Do you also *give* coats?" I asked.

"What do you mean?"

I rolled my eyes, slowly. I was glad no one else was there to see the exchange. The kid was dense. If I did fire him, I'd probably be doing him a favour. It would keep him from getting killed in the near future by a less gregarious boss. I grinned, as I thought of myself as the nicest alternative in a world of thugs.

"Do you also *give* coats?" I repeated. "You know. If I hand over this little green piece of paper, can I get my jacket back?"

His face went red, and he grabbed the ticket from my outstretched hand.

I waited as patiently as I could manage. I wanted to get home, drink a bit more and watch some PVRed horror movies. What would the nervous kid would think of that?

Big bad boss, cuddled up under a blanket while taking in a classic slasher flick, I smiled. *He'd probably never believe it, even if I told him that's what I was going to do. Unless I told him I was taking notes for work, of course...*

I was riding the high of the information Yun had given me when I made the decision to come down to the club. Getting a drink and maybe even socializing to celebrate had seemed like a good idea. And I had actually thought the bar was an especially appropriate place to celebrate my first break in finding Colin's murderer. After all, it had been my brother's little investment. I had wholeheartedly opposed it at the time, of course. I'd been furious when I'd found out what he'd done with his inheritance.

"You couldn't pick something more worthwhile?" I fumed.

"I want to do something I care about," Colin told me.

"And you care about what? Dancing? Drinking? Wasting Mom's money?"

He sighed. "That's your biggest problem, John. You still think of the money as hers. It's not hers. It's ours. She left it to us for a reason."

"And that reason was to go to school," I reminded him angrily.

"No," Colin argued. "It was to give us a chance at life."

I growled, feeling totally exasperated as I usually did when dealing with this particular topic.

"You're too much like Dad," my brother said. "You don't think money is for spending. At least Mom knew that is what it's for."

"Mom grew up wealthy," I told him. "She never had to think about where the next dollar was coming from. Dad had to work for every last goddamned dime."

Colin threw up his hands.

"Fine!" he shouted. "I'll go after a career, too."

"Good," I replied, feeling victorious.

"Good," he said back.

But that was before he'd told me his career choice

was going to be the same as mine, and before it had gone and gotten him killed.

And when he'd died, I'd been stuck with the club. I wanted to sell it at first, I really did. But I couldn't make myself do it. So even though I hadn't approved of it at all when Colin had purchased it, I'd made an honest effort to turn the bar into something worthwhile.

Truthfully, owning it didn't hurt my reputation, either. And it did make quite a bit of money. I felt guilty, knowing that Colin had been right.

I had wanted to enjoy my evening, thinking I was getting closer to finding out what the tattoo drawing had meant, and to finding out who had killed him.

Then I had spotted the girl, the slim, blonde one from the tattoo parlour, out on the dance floor. With the brunette's obvious physical charms out of the way, I could see that the blonde really was quite pretty. Maybe even beautiful. I watched her shake in time to the music, and decided there was no *maybe* about it. I sipped my drink and smiled as I looked at her. It was obvious she wasn't usually much of a dancer, not because she didn't have rhythm, just because she didn't have the wanton abandon of the usual club girls. I even went so far as toying with the idea of approaching her before I reminded myself that the last thing I needed was a distraction.

Then Monato was there, all over her.

I put my drink down carefully when I saw him. The man set my teeth on edge. I knew all about his so-called business—dealing women to the high rolling card players and drug dealers who were always lurking nearby. And dealing drugs to those same women to keep them under his thumb.

Creepy little shit. I watched him gyrate against the blonde.

She *had* been smiling, and laughing. Then all of sudden she wasn't. When Monato grabbed her, I had acted without thinking, rushing to rescue her and to send the other man packing.

I cursed myself for doing it. Playing superhero was *not* in my repertoire of tricks. Being in the habit of saving strangers would tend to give my clients the wrong idea about me. So even as I'd done it, I'd regretted it.

Dumb move, Seever, I told myself again.

That was why I needed to get away from the club as quickly as possible. And there I was, waiting for the kid to get my coat.

"What the Hell is taking so long," I muttered. "It's just a jacket."

I needed to get *out*—away from the odd looks I'd received from my crew as they'd watched me kiss the girl's hand. What had possessed me to do that anyway? With the way things were going I'd probably have to justify it later. I'd ordered another drink to drown my irritation, but it had only increased my frustration.

And when Monato had cornered me after our little exchange, it had taken everything in my power to not strangle him, then and there.

"The girl really yours?" he'd asked.

"Why are you in my club, Monato?" I replied.

"Checking out the competition," he told me.

"You're not exactly what I'd call competition," I said coldly. "Why are you interested in the girl?"

"She's just my friend's type."

Monato's laugh set my teeth on edge once again.

"You've got friends?" I countered.

He shrugged. "A few."

I rolled my eyes. His whole crew was never further than three feet away.

"So she's not yours?" Monato persisted.

"Everything in this club is mine. And she happens to be just my type, too," I stated.

"That's not an answer."

"Yes," I sighed. "She's my girl. In every sense of the word. Maybe soon to be something even more."

"That so? Funny how I've actually never seen you with a girl," Monato said. "Me, I've got a new one each week."

"That's what I hear, too," I replied. "You have a hard time getting them to stay?"

Monato's face had gone dark. I wasn't normally so mouthy—it just made good business sense to play nice, even with him—and I tried, unsuccessfully to back it up a bit.

"I'm getting bored of this little pissing contest," I told him. "Pack your friends up. Stay away from my girl. And get out of my club."

He'd stomped off in his typical fashion.

I shook my head irritably and hoped I still had some whiskey in my apartment. I was going to drink to the point of numbness and take tomorrow off.

"Hey!" I called to the coat check kid.

No answer. I pulled a key from my pocket and let myself into the abyss of a cloakroom. There was still no sign of the kid. The hair on the back of my neck stood up, and I sensed something wasn't quite right. I went very still and waited. Cool air wafted in from somewhere, and a groan came from up ahead.

"Christ," I complained, knowing already what I'd find as I stepped further into the room.

The kid was lying on the floor with a trickle of blood oozing from his forehead. He struggled to open his eyes, and I grabbed a random coat to prop him up. I kneeled down and put the makeshift pillow under him.

"You gotta be more careful," I told him. "What's your name, buddy?"

"Monato," the kid mumbled.

"What?" I thought I'd misheard him.

"Monato," he repeated, a little more clearly.

"Your name is *Monato*?" I asked harshly.

If some idiot has gone and hired a relative of that jerk-off, I thought. *I don't know what I'm gonna do.*

The kid shook his head and groaned again. "No. Not me. Monato came through. He had a girl over his shoulder."

"He what?"

I let the kid flop down onto the coat. I stood up quickly and swept the room with my eyes. I cursed myself for not seeing it before. The door between the bar storeroom and the coat check room was wide open, and the emergency exit at the very back, hidden behind a sea of jackets, was also open, just a crack.

I knew without asking which girl Monato had over his shoulder. There was only one reason he would've taken her, and it had everything to do with getting back at me for taking her from him in the first place.

Chapter Five

I could smell garbage and filth. It made my skin crawl, and it made my consciousness refuse to surface. It flung me backwards to the time before I lost Jeannette, and I fought that even more than I fought to wake myself up.

I lost the battle, though, and I was suddenly sixteen years old, trapped in a back alley.

"What's up?" said the haggard man blocking my way.

I should've been scared, and somewhere inside I was. But this was what I had been running toward while running from the despair that had taken over my life when my sister died.

I inhaled deeply, breathing in the stench of rotting food and unwashed skin. I thought maybe that second stink was me, but I dismissed it as I met the homeless man's nervous gaze.

"Do your worst," I told him.

He frowned, like he was expecting me to say anything but that.

"You can't hurt me," I added.

I'm already broken.

"Hurt you?"

I nodded and he laughed falsely.

"Kid, I'm not going to hurt you. I'm just hungry."

"This is my spot," I told him, and gestured to the

ragged blanket and pile of clothes behind the dumpster.

I'd been sleeping there for maybe four nights, but it was longest I'd stayed anywhere in God knows how long, and I had turned sixteen there, just the day before. I felt an irrational ownership of the place.

He put his hands up and backed away. I relaxed, just for a second, and then he was on me, pinning my arms to my sides. Another man, whom I hadn't noticed before, came at me, too, and went through my pockets roughly.

"Twenty dollars!" he announced gleefully, exposing his meth-rotted teeth.

And that's when I got mad. I kicked out blindly, and hit something solid—a shin, or a stomach, or an arm, it didn't matter which—and the man grunted. I ground my teeth together and clenched all of my muscles. Weeks of eating poorly had weakened me, but I was still stronger than my captor.

"Don't you know what drugs do to you?!"

My screaming must have scared him, because suddenly I was free, and he was cowering at my feet.

"That's right!" I hollered. "You're bigger than I am, and older than I am, but your stupid goddamned dependency has turned you into a scared little thief!"

In my head, I knew I wasn't really angry at him, but I went on anyway. He tried to scurry away, and it made me feel powerful and in control and I stomped after him, still yelling.

"What do you think you could've done with your life?! Would your mom be proud, to see you robbing a teenager of her last twenty bucks? I doubt it!"

The man kept moving back, and it finally struck me as odd. Especially when I realized he wasn't looking at me, but over my shoulder. I turned, and my mouth dropped open, just a little bit. A cold-eyed police officer in a blue uniform was watching us with curiosity. His hand was resting casually on his holstered weapon.

"Oh, no," I whispered.

A furious amount of shuffling and dirty blur running past let me know the would-be robber had bolted.

"How old are you?" the cop asked.

I shook my head. There was no point in answering. I didn't even look my *own* age—there would be no convincing him I was eighteen.

"Dispatch, I'm going to need social services," he announced into the radio attached to his shoulder.

Too late, I moved. He was fast, and his arms— stronger and far less relenting than those of the homeless man—came around me. I punched and kicked, but it did no good.

My six months of freedom were over, and the foster system was waiting.

I tried to drag myself out of the dream. It was dark, and it still smelled like garbage. And I thought I might be hanging upside down. My head bump-bump-bumped along in an alarming way.

Why won't it stop?

A bunch of male voices, competed for supremacy.

"Shit, she's waking up," someone said.

The chemical-laden rag came up over my face, and I faded out again.

Chapter Six

I ran. I didn't stop to call for help.

This is your fault! I shouted at myself. *If you hadn't jumped in there when he was dancing with her, he'd probably have left well enough alone!*

I shoved down the internal voice with a snarl. It wouldn't matter too much whose fault it was if I couldn't get to her quickly enough.

I burst through the exterior door and surveyed either direction. To my left was a warren of alleys, riddled with garbage bins and rats and people of questionable character. If I was kidnapping someone, it's the way I would've gone. But Monato wasn't me. He was probably the kind of man who liked things easy. I glanced to my right. It was dark, but just around the corner was a narrow space between two buildings that led out to the main road. I took off in that direction.

My instincts were right.

As I reached the street, I spied Monato and two of his thugs huddled against the exterior wall of the restaurant a few doors down from the club. I shook my head at their audacity. And at their idiocy.

A blonde girl was hanging over one of the men's shoulders, and she was clearly unconscious. They hadn't even bothered to cover her up.

What was their plan if they got caught? I wondered. *What if the police drove by, as they often did, and saw them standing there?*

No self-respecting cop—hell, no self-respecting person—would believe a stupid story about the girl having had too much to drink

I stepped onto the sidewalk and did my best to appear invisible. No easy task when you're my size. I kept close to the sides of the buildings as I moved along with my head down.

How did a guy like Monato suddenly become my main target, when there were so many other more worthwhile pursuits?

I knew the answer. Or at least partly. I was more than just the girl tonight. I didn't like how Monato made his money. I didn't like how he was always rubbing it in people's faces. He was nothing more than a lowlife pimp. There was something else. Something beyond the asshole factor. The more I interacted with him, the more I knew it, even if I couldn't quite figure out what *it* was.

As I got close enough I could really see the blonde's face. It was her, of course. One of Monato's men—the one not carrying the girl—caught sight of me as I approached them.

"Hey!" he shouted.

I stepped up casually and clocked him on the side of the head with one of my fists. He crumpled to the ground, and the other man looked down in surprise before he turned toward me.

"Give her over," I commanded.

He hesitated, and for a second I really thought he was going to give me the girl. Monato grabbed his arm.

"You weren't kidding about keeping her, then?" he sneered.

"Did I look like I was kidding?" I asked.

"I'm just surprised is all," Monato said. "You seem to have so very little interest in anything but kicking me out of your club on a regular basis."

"So stop coming in," I suggested.

"No."

I bristled. "Give me the girl."

"No."

"This is a new low for you, isn't it?" I persisted. "Don't you usually just hook them on drugs so they continue to need you?

A dark sedan pulled up in front of us, and the door swung open. I moved to block it.

"I would love to stay here and further discuss my shortcomings. Maybe negotiate a deal. But I'm afraid our ride is already here," Monato told me with an obnoxious shrug.

He pulled out a tiny revolver and waved it casually in my direction before instructing his thug to load the girl into the trunk of the car.

"You won't shoot me out here in front of my own club," I said. "Even you aren't that stupid."

"No," he agreed. "But I might shoot *her*. No one will give a shit but you. And if anything happens to me, I've made sure my driver will take her somewhere inconveniently hard to find."

I considered his words. He was just barely shrewd enough to have made that arrangement ahead of time.

"I'll have you followed," I warned.

"I know," Monato said with a smile.

He slammed the trunk shut and gestured for me to move. I snarled, and made to get out of his way, and then a hand reached out from inside the car and tapped the back of my leg.

"Get in," hissed a familiar voice.

I didn't hesitate. I bent myself in half and fell into the sedan. The tires squealed and the car took off down the road.

It took me a second to right myself and close the door.

"Jesus, Billy!" I swore. "Why didn't you just tell me it was you?"

The older man grinned, which made his scarred face go from macabre to terrifying. I punched him in the arm.

"I saw you kiss some poor girl…on the *hand* of all places," he replied. "And then you had a loud fight with our buddy, Monato. So I followed his guys. Took his driver out, and borrowed this luxurious little ride. Waited until I thought you might need me. But really…You looked like you were doing all right."

"Like hell I did."

"Anyway, I figured you didn't want to go without the girl."

I shook my head. "So you were chancing my life to save some stranger?"

"The only chance I ever took was agreeing to do this job with you," he replied. "You're the one risking your life for the girl."

I didn't argue. Billy was my most trusted guy, and the only one who could get away with speaking his mind—to a certain extent anyway.

"Where are we going?" I wanted to know.

"Hopefully somewhere safer than your club."

I sighed and let him drive. I had enough thoughts tumbling through my head to keep me occupied. And I needed to stop letting Monato get to me if I wanted to do the job I'd come to do. I had put in too much time getting where I was. I couldn't let it slip away over some girl I didn't know.

Billy navigated the streets quickly, and when he flicked the lights off and cruised into an unfamiliar underground parking lot, my tension level spiked again.

"Relax," Billy said. "We're just going to stop so we can take the girl out of the trunk. Then you can find a better place to hide out."

Hiding out. Not my style. It made me irritable.

"You'll need to carry her yourself," Billy told me as we exited the car. "I've got a bad elbow."

I rolled my eyes. He ignored my look and opened the trunk.

I stared down at her for just a moment, realizing again that she was beautiful. Her skin was porcelain white, and her hair was fine, and it looked soft I had to hold in a ridiculous urge to reach out and stroke it. Her head rolled to one side, and she let out a loud snore. It made me laugh before I could stop myself.

"Hurry it up," Billy urged.

I bent down and put one hand under her knees and the other under her shoulders. I lifted her carefully, and cradled her still form against my body. I don't know if it was her apparent vulnerability, or just the closeness of her—it had been so long since I'd let anyone near me like that—but my chest compressed involuntarily.

I carried her over to the waiting car. Thankfully, it was one of our vehicles. I didn't bother to ask why Billy had it there as I placed the girl carefully in the back seat and covered her with my coat.

"Billy," I said in an uncharacteristically husky

voice. "I'm gonna leave her with you and double back to the club in a cab. I won't be long. I just need to make sure we weren't followed and sort out a few things."

The older man nodded once. He respectfully didn't ask what those things were, and didn't give me any flack for not trusting his evasive driving skills. I was glad I didn't have to admit the girl's presence had unnerved me to the point of needing to get a breather.

I headed up and out to the street where I hailed a cab.

Twenty minutes tops, I told myself, because as much as I wanted to clear my head, I wanted to be near the girl even more.

Chapter Seven

This is the beginning of the worst hangover in the world.

My head throbbed, and there was a thick pit of nothing but nausea where my stomach should be.

I could hear voices again, and I mumbled at Blair to turn down the TV while mentally cursing her for feeding me such an excessive amount of alcohol. For a second, it got quiet, and I settled in thankfully, trying to go back to sleep. But the voices got louder once again, and I wondered why she would turn the program up when I asked her to turn it down.

Doesn't she know I'm sick?

The television was so loud that it felt like the characters were in the room with me.

"What's his plan, now?" said a gruff, male voice.

There was no response to the question, and I decided he was either talking to himself, or talking on the phone.

Weird, that the program isn't playing both sides on the conversation.

"No, seriously," the gruff voice continued after a moment. "Now that he's got her here...It could jeopardize everything."

The words should've meant something to me. I couldn't quite remember why. Was it a movie I had seen? A program Blair had made me watch before? It didn't sound like her usual reality TV show babble.

Someone leaned over me, and I tried to say my friend's name. It came out as a gurgle. Or at least I thought it did.

Must still be drunk, I concluded.

But I felt so sick, and I had such a terrible taste in my mouth.

I can't be drunk and hungover at the same time. Can I?

I heard paper shuffling and a car door slammed. The noise reverberated in my head and I thought I might throw up. I fought down the urge.

"Christ, Billy," someone swore, and the voice was almost—but not quite—familiar. "What the hell is this?"

"The girl," answered the gruff voice, presumably Billy.

"Yeah, I see that. But why is her stuff everywhere? Looks like a purse exploded in here."

"Needed an ID," Billy replied.

I must've watched this already, I thought drowsily.

"An ID? You kidding?"

"No."

"Did you think about a little thing called the Internet, Billy? I got a hell of a lot more than an ID without doing *this.*"

"Yeah?"

"Yeah."

"I don't happen to have a Wifi connection here, all right? And I've been waiting for you for an hour."

I tried to sort out what was going on as the men argued, but it was too hard for me to follow. Their voices blurred together and I really just wished Blair would turn it off.

"Wasn't smart."

"Suppose I just let them have her?"

"Really not our problem."

"When did you become such an asshole?"

"I'm not an asshole. I'm the one who helped you. But this is business. And we're not gonna be in business for long if we don't get rid of her."

"Where's the Doc? Didn't you call him?"

"Relax. He's on his way back."

"He was here already?"

"Well, I sure as shit didn't put the hole in her hand."

"The what?!"

"The IV port."

"He wants to hydrate her."

"No."

There was silence then, except for the sound of someone tapping something, again and again.

Was it Blair? My friend wasn't usually so noisy. *Why is she doing that? I'd kill for some water.*

The pause in the fighting continued, and then one of them asked, "So who did *you* ID her as?"

"I found her driver's license. She's Cass Sternlight."

The sound of my name brought me to attention.

It's not the TV, I realized with sudden apprehension as the events of the night surfaced in my groggy brain.

I clearly remembered Monato and the chemical-soaked towel. Everything after was more or less a blank. But my head hurt, and my lungs were sore. I had a strange, sharp pain in one of my hands, and I felt a bit like death warmed over.

The IV. I wanted to scream.. *They put an IV in my hand!*

I cringed involuntarily against whatever padding was beneath my body, trying to shrink into oblivion. Then I froze. I didn't want them to realize I was awake.

Where am I? I need to figure it out.

I was afraid to open my eyes, so instead I tried to take careful inventory of what I could feel.

My back stung where the tattoo was, but aside from that and my pounding head, I wasn't physically hurt. I could still taste the acetone-like inhalant that had knocked me out, and I wondered what it was they had used to soak the towel. I wiggled my fingers. They tingled ever so slightly, and so did my feet. But I was quite warm, and something soft covered most of my body.

A blanket, I decided, grasping to understand some part of my surroundings. *I must be under a blanket. And I'm on a...What? A couch, maybe.*

My stinging back was pressed against something firm, and I could feel the springs under the rest of my body.

I took a risk and opened my eyes ever so slightly.

It was almost dark, but I realized instantly that I wasn't in a building and I wasn't on a couch at all. I was in the backseat of a car. I could make out the outlines of the men who'd been discussing my fate. One of them was sitting in the driver's seat, which he had tilted most of the way back. The other was in the passenger's seat, and I was pretty sure he was drumming on the dashboard. From what I could see, neither of them looked—or sounded like—Monato or any of his friends.

A rush of cool air brushed my face as one of the rear doors opened, and I quickly closed my eyes. Someone shifted my body, and joined me in the backseat.

"Hey, Doc," greeted the gruff-voiced man.

Billy, I reminded myself, trying to keep everything straight.

The sound of a lighter flicking echoed through the car, and a second or two later, the scent of cigarette smoke wafted through as well. I inhaled—subtly— because for just a moment, the smell of it relieved me of the acrid taste in my mouth.

"I wish you wouldn't do that around my patient," complained the doctor.

"Your patient?" Billy replied scornfully. "Didn't they take away your license?"

"I surrendered it voluntarily," the doctor stated calmly.

A cool hand rested on my forehead, and someone tugged at the back of my aching hand.

The IV port, I remembered, and tried to keep still as the unlicensed doctor adjusted it.

"I could hydrate her now," he said. "But she's still not going to feel very well when she comes to. I'd like to give her some anti-nauseant through the IV."

"No."

The disagreement came from the man in the passenger seat, and I really thought I should be able to place his voice.

"I can just put it right into the line, and it'll probably keep her knocked out," the doctor ventured.

"I said no." The familiar-ish voice was impatient. "I want her lucid, and soon."

"C'mon," Billy said. "He went to the trouble of getting the IV in. And *you* called *him*."

"To take a look. Nothing more."

Both Billy and the Doc sighed.

There was another tug on my hand, and I kept very still.

"Let go," commanded the man who wasn't Billy or the doctor.

My hand dropped loosely back to my side. There was silence for a moment, and then the man sighed.

"I've got some dissolvable anti-nauseant in my first aid kit. I'll give her some of that, okay?"

There was some shuffling, and I felt hands on my face. Soap-scented fingers pulled on my mouth very gently, and a pill landed on my tongue. I resisted the urge to spit it out as it dissolved.

"Do you think she's actually connected to Monato?" the doctor asked.

"No," the familiar-sounding man answered. "No way."

"Why keep her here then?" the doctor wondered out loud.

"She's just some goddamned chick John couldn't live without," replied Billy with more than a hint of frustration. "Chivalry's not fucking dead, I guess."

"What is wrong with you guys? Have you been doing this so long that…" The familiar voice—John—trailed off, exasperated.

"Doing *what*?" Billy asked coldly at the same time as the doctor said, "Of course not."

"You don't sound like yourself," Billy added.

"Look, she's not a coincidence. She's not a chick. She's a *person*. Who needed our help. And if she's awake, she now knows your name, Billy, and mine. Might as well add yours to the mix." Even in my increasingly hazy state, I could tell that he sounded awfully pissed off. "Cass Sternlight, I'd like to formally introduce you to the doctor formerly known as Ramirez."

"Either way, John, she's your problem now," Billy said, and his cigarette sizzled as he butted it out. "This is as far as I'm going. I'm not sticking around to see the shit hit the fan. I'm out."

I was getting really sleepy again, but I forced my eyes open, just a sliver.

From underneath my lashes, I watched the gruff man move his seat up and toss a set of keys to John before climbing out. The car door slammed shut.

"Stay with her," John commanded to the Doc after a moment, and he followed Billy out.

My eyes didn't want to stay open, and I sighed audibly.

"You there, miss?" the doctor asked.

He sounded very nearly kind, but I couldn't have answered him, even if I'd been inclined to do so. He sighed, too, and placed a gentle hand on my forehead once again.

"I'll take care of you," he said, then I drifted off.

There was a loud screech, and I heard John's voice again, tense and hurried.

"Pack it in, Doc," he ordered. "And take out that damned needle. We've got a problem."

I tried desperately to keep conscious, but even as I felt the IV yanked out of my hand, and sensed that blood was dripping from the wound there, I couldn't hold on.

Chapter Eight

Things were going from bad to worse, and then worse again. As I rushed to get through town at a speed that made even me cringe, I wavered between blaming myself and blaming the girl—Cass Sternlight.

I'd only been out of the car for a minute—just trying to talk Billy into getting back in—when I'd spied the lights of another car. At first I'd ignored them as I'd talked to the older man.

"C'mon," I cajoled. "Do I ever steer you wrong?"

He grunted.

"I'm just trying to do what's right," I said.

"Since when?"

"Since always."

"So you're gonna forget your personal vendetta for the first pretty face that walks through your door?"

He was being sarcastic, and I made myself brush it off. Billy knew better than anyone that nothing short of my own death would make me give up on finding my brother's killer.

"She didn't just walk through my door. I dragged her kicking and screaming," I told him.

"You carried her while she snored," Billy reminded me.

I rolled my eyes.

"I'm still on the job," I assured him.

Then the car lights had flashed again, and we both

turned toward the winding ramp that led down to where we were parked.

"Monato followed us," I muttered. "Clever little bastard."

"Fuck," Billy replied, for once sounding angrier than I did.

We' jumped back into the car, and I turned the ignition on, turned the lights off, and eased the car through the lot until I'd hit the service ramp on the other side of the underground structure. We made it to the exit and the road, but my blood pressure was still up, and I hadn't made a decision about what my next move was going to be.

The whiskey had finally worn off, and I couldn't help but wonder how much it had influenced my actions tonight.

"If you have any sense left, John, you'll drop her at the address listed on her license, and move on," Billy told me.

"No," I replied coldly.

"But John…" The doctor said, sounding uncertain.

"What?" I snapped. "I can't just leave her somewhere for Monato to take."

"Under almost every other circumstance, I would agree with you. But in this case, I'm not sure you're thinking straight," he told me nervously.

A growl built up in my throat, mostly because I'd been thinking the same thing. I refused to back down. I was starting to regret having called the doctor in the first place. Ramirez was soft, often simpering, and always self-serving. It was why he'd been asked to surrender his license—he made his decisions based on what was good for *him*, not what was good for his patients. If Cass Sternlight hadn't been so still, and I'd known what to do for her myself, I wouldn't have asked for his help at all.

"Under *any* other circumstance, I would toss you out of the car without stopping to think about it," I said quietly. "You should be thanking God that I still have the girl. That's what's keeping you in one piece."

That shut him up, at least momentarily.

I slowed for a yellow, waited impatiently through the red, and moved on wordlessly when it became a green. I kept driving, and tried to work out a plan.

Billy opened his mouth several times, thought better of whatever he'd been going to say, then closed it again.

I wasn't going anywhere near my apartment, or anywhere else I could be found on a regular basis. I figured even Monato was smart enough to station people there.

I cringed when I considered what his men might do to the old man at the front desk in my apartment building. If they questioned him in an attempt to find out where I'd gone…I really hated the thought of being indirectly responsible for any harm that came to innocent people.

Oh, really? I said to myself sarcastically. *That's not at all obvious.*

I made a mental note to check on the desk attendant later, and kept moving.

We were getting low on gas, but I was too cautious of a man—at least when it came to my business life—to stop at any of the stations in town. And I obviously hadn't been being careful enough so far.

"What's the plan?" Billy finally asked when the

fuel light began to blink.

I stared at the glowing E and was struck by a sudden inspiration. I glanced in the rearview mirror, pulled over and handed Billy my credit card.

"Get out," I said.

Both Billy and the Doc looked at me incredulously.

"We're in the middle of the highway," Billy pointed out.

"Call a cab," I told him. "I really think it's better if I take her somewhere safe. And alone. Monato can follow the card instead of me."

For a second, Billy seemed like he was going to argue, but I shook my head, and the two men got out slowly. I glanced at the pretty blonde in the backseat. Without Ramirez crowding her, she looked smaller and even more vulnerable. It made me feel like I'd made the right decision.

I pulled back onto the road, and I didn't look back at the two men I'd abandoned.

I kept going until I hit the highway, glad to have thought of the hotel. It was huge, out of the way, and except for a few renovated rooms, near to uninhabitable.

Damn. I realized that the very thing that made it suitable for hiding, also made it unsuitable for a long-term stay. *I'm going to need to stop.*

I drove a little further, ignoring the angrily blinking fuel light until I spotted a sign advertising an out-of-the-way, twenty-four hour grocery and gas. I stopped for some supplies. I had no choice but to leave the girl in the car, and I had to fight to keep myself from running through the store as I picked up the things I might need. Food. Drinks. Toiletries.

"Like I'm taking a goddamned vacation," I muttered.

My heart hammered guiltily as I paid.

"You all right?" the bored cashier asked.

I nodded, cursing myself for being so transparent, and for letting myself be someone who would be remembered. How had I made it this far in my life of crime?

"I need gas," I told her curtly.

"Pump is down."

I suppressed a frustrated sigh and paid the girl in cash for the other stuff.

When I got back into the car, my hands clenched the steering wheel. I couldn't force them to release, even as I pulled the inconspicuous sedan onto the road.

"Thirty clicks," I muttered at the gas gauge. "That's all I ask."

I didn't breathe easily until I caught sight of the largely hidden sign. Its signature E—broken and unlit—proclaimed that we'd reached the Empress Hotel.

I drove to the back lot slowly, with the lights out, and parked the car beside the rundown laundry facility. I was glad I had decided not to have it levelled. It provided the perfect cover, and my car would go unnoticed, at least for a little while.

I glanced at my watch. The live-in security detail I'd hired to patrol the perimeter of the hotel itself would've finished his latest rounds twenty minutes earlier. I had about an hour until he came around again. Plenty of time to let him know I'd become a guest. I doubted I could fully trust him, but I would have to, at least until I figured out a solid plan.

I opened the back door and lifted the girl out. I

cradled her against my chest while balancing the weight of the two grocery bags on my arms. I paused for a second.

Would I be able to manage the trek over to the hotel without dropping her?

"You'd better be worth all this trouble," I said.

She sighed softly and settled more comfortably into my grip. One of her arms came up automatically in her sleep, and she bent it at the elbow. Her hand was resting gently on my collar bone. I looked down, and my body decided—all on its own—that the sight of her delicate fingers, curled possessively against my chest was more than worth it.

I swallowed thickly and told myself to move.

Chapter Nine

The lights went on without warning, waking me up and causing pain to shoot through my eyes and deep into my skull. I made a small, involuntary noise, and I saw the man named John turn toward me right before I covered my whole face with my hands. He didn't move, and neither did I. The room was quiet except for the sound of my own breathing. My heart rate increased uncomfortably as I realized I was *alone* with the big, angry-sounding man.

"Welcome back, Cass Sternlight," he greeted, and I really thought I should be able to place his voice.

"It's not Sternlight," I corrected before I could stop myself.

"Isn't it?" He gave me a little smile. "Are you…undercover?"

I considered not answering, but I didn't want to aggravate him any further. I hadn't fully been able to see him before I covered my face, but he had looked big. And dangerous. I shivered involuntarily and replied without taking my hands away from my eyes.

"No, I'm not undercover."

He was quiet again for a moment, and I could feel him giving me a once-over.

"Divorced," he stated.

"Annulled," I corrected.

"I see."

We were both silent.

"Could you possibly turn out the lights?" I asked finally.

His feet hit the floor hard as he walked across the room. I sighed in relief as the switch clicked and it went dark. I uncovered my eyes. John was standing in front of me. He had a glass in his hand. I squinted up at him. He didn't just sound familiar, he *looked* it, too, though I couldn't remember from where.

"It's water," he said, offering me the glass. "Drink it slowly, or you'll probably throw it up."

I struggled to sit up, and the room swam.

I might throw up anyway. I accepted the glass, and took a tiny, hesitant sip.

It was cool, but not cold, and it washed away a bit more of the bad taste in my mouth. I made a face.

"Ether," John told me.

"What?"

"That's what they used to knock you out."

"Oh."

I didn't know what else to say. How did he know what they used? Had he helped them?

"Doc told me that's what it was," he said irritably, as if he had heard my thoughts. "I'm not in the habit of drugging women."

I reddened, and avoided meeting his eyes. He didn't have the same menacing presence as Monato and his buddies, but that really didn't mean much.

Unless he saved you from them, I said to myself.

Then it clicked.

"The gun!" I gasped out loud.

John was the same brown-eyed stranger who had pretended to be my…what? Boyfriend? No, not quite.

He had identified me as his property.

"It's locked up right this second." He rolled his eyes.

"The gun is?"

"Yes."

"Where?" My face heated up again. "Sorry. That's none of my business."

John shrugged and his eyes softened a touch as gave me another assessing once-over. "It's fine. Fairly sure you couldn't use it even if you could get to it. I'm keeping it in a portable safe under the bed. It's always secure unless I'm going out without it."

"Do you do that often?"

He gave me a penetrating look. "You ask a lot of questions for a girl who's been kidnapped."

I flushed. "Is that what this is? Did you kidnap me?"

He grinned, and laughed out loud. "I guess I did."

"And what are you going to *do* with me?"

He raised an eyebrow, and I looked down at my hands quickly. I hadn't meant it to sound that way, but when I saw his reaction, I was instantly very aware of John's appearance.

He was tall—well over six feet—with broad shoulders. He had a strong jaw and straight teeth, framed by lips that were just the right kind of full. His hair was very short, and dark brown with just enough gray to be sexy. And his eyes were like chocolate.

Mocha, I heard Blair say in my head, and I agreed with her, just this once. John's eyes were mocha-brown.

"Oh, no," I muttered. "Blair."

"Your friend is fine," he assured me. "It's you I'm worried about."

"You should be worried about *her*," I told him. "When she finds out I'm missing, she's gonna freak. She'll probably call the police."

"She won't. And if she did, they wouldn't find us."

He sounded utterly certain, and it made me feel really frightened for the first time.

"Why not?" I gulp nervously.

He didn't answer right away, and his intense stare made me look away.

I examined the room instead, trying to figure out if I could discern where we might me. It had the impersonal decor of a hotel room. There was a little table—it was the only one in the room, and it had just the two chairs. In the corner of the room, I could see a tiny kitchenette. It was functional only, with a small fridge, a microwave, a single sink, and a two-burner hotplate. There was a white door at the end of the room, and without even looking inside, I could imagine the bedroom—two twin beds, one night stand in the middle, and a TV on top of an armoire.

Maybe there might be a picture of the ocean on one of the walls, just to keep it from being too bland, I reasoned.

I turned my attention back to John. He was following my gaze, and a small smile was playing on his lips.

"This really isn't that kind of kidnapping, Cass not-Sternlight," he said almost playfully. "Though your presence does me make wonder."

"I wasn't…" I stopped myself before I could say anything stupid.

He smiled, and I realized with him looking at me like that with the playful glint in his chocolate eyes, and amusement reflected in the set of his full lips, I wouldn't be able to do it. In fact, I was *more* likely to say a few stupid things. So I resolved not to say anything at all, except in response to a direct question.

John narrowed his mocha-brown eyes at me as if he could see my sudden determination. "You were asking me why not?"

"Why not what?"

I told myself I couldn't remember what I'd been asking because of the aftereffects of the ether, and not because of his handsome face and innuendo.

He kidnapped you! I reminded myself. *He is* not *that handsome.*

But he was. He had perfect cheekbones, a muscular torso, and well-shaped limbs. His eyes were intense and sharp, making me think he was probably smart, too. His mouth curled up, just on the left side when he was talking.

He's talking.

I blushed as I realized I'd been so busy checking him out that I hadn't quite caught what he was saying.

What is wrong *with me?*

He was looking at me like he was waiting for me to speak.

"Could you repeat that?" I said, feeling dumber than I ever had in my whole life.

"Are you okay?"

"I've been kidnapped," I reminded him, and he laughed.

"I was just saying that you were asking why the police won't find us."

"Why won't the police find us?" I replied in a purposely automatic voice.

John's smile widened. "Because I'm a dangerous man, Cass. And I don't want to be found."

He excused himself politely, and I stared at his wide shoulders as he disappeared into the bedroom.

Chapter Ten

I wasn't being menacing on purpose. Just the opposite in fact. I could tell from her face that she was still at least a little intimidated. I hadn't truly sat and talked to someone outside of the business in what seemed like a very long time. And since the girl opened her eyes...I was confused.

I was unused to answering for anyone but myself. I wasn't accustomed to being questioned, either. The girl *did* ask a lot of questions. I sat down on the bed and put my head in my hands. I had dismissed Billy and the doctor because I thought it would be safer. I'd assumed it would be easier to explain the situation to the girl if we were alone.

Then she had asked me if I had kidnapped her, and she'd asked about the gun, and my God, she really was beautiful. I'd caught myself flirting with her. Or trying to flirt with her. I wasn't very good at it. I was out of practice.

It wasn't what I was supposed to be doing anyway I reminded myself for the tenth time. I sent Billy a text, letting him know we were okay. It was funny to type the word "we" instead of just my usual "I". Had Billy noticed it, too? Probably. He was observant because he was paid to be.

His reply was almost instantaneous and condescending in its paternal tone.

You kids have fun. Be careful.

I groaned at my phone, and stood up. I plastered a smile on my face, and went out to face her again. I resolved to keep my distance and to think of her as just another job.

"I'm starving. You hungry?" I asked brightly, and I was happy when she nodded almost imperceptibly, because it meant I could gather my thoughts while I cooked.

I knew without checking that she was looking at me as I worked. I wasn't used to an audience, and I tried to ignore her. But I could feel her slate-gray eyes on my back.

A plan was forming in my mind, but I didn't like where it was leading. I had a deep need to protect her, and there were only two ways I could think of doing it. The first option was to carry on the farce of my claim on her. It would mean exposing her to my business associates, and just the *thought* of bringing her any further into my world made me nervous.

The second option was far less intrusive, and it would keep her under the radar. It would be safer. But it would also mean holding her hostage. I didn't think that would go over well.

She'd been curious and cautious so far, but not hostile.

I chopped the red pepper in front of me with entirely more fervour than was necessary.

If you choose the hostage route, not only will she not like it...She probably won't like you *much, either,* said a small voice in my head.

I sliced through an onion angrily, annoyed that the thought had even crossed my mind.

With the exception of maybe Billy, most of the people who ran in my circle didn't like me. But they respected me, and keeping it that way was my primary goal.

Secondary goal after finding Colin's killer, I corrected mentally. *And carting the girl around would interfere with my ability to pursue the tattoo artist—on a large scale.*

My hand slipped as I realized I had almost forgotten about my big tip from Yun, and I was equally surprised that I had forgotten to factor it into my plans in the first place.

"You're bleeding!"

I looked down. Cass was right. I had been so distracted that I hadn't even felt the knife make the slice.

She was beside me then, wrapping a cloth around my thumb and putting pressure there. She was a little unsteady on her feet—probably from the combo of ether and anti-nauseant—and she steadied herself by gripping my arm as she held the wound shut. I inhaled sharply. I could smell the chemical odour of the ether, and the lingering scent of cigarette smoke from being in the car with Billy. But I could also smell her shampoo, and another, subtle perfume. She squeezed my wound firmly, and when she shifted slightly to keep the pressure even, her hip brushed my thigh.

I had a sudden vision of me, lifting her up onto the counter, pulling her top over her head and…I stopped myself before I could get any further. I yanked my hand away.

"I'm fine," I told her curtly. "And I don't want to burn the food."

I kept my eyes off her as she went back to the couch. As much as I loathed the idea of dragging her into my seedy world, I was really hoping she would choose option number one.

She watched me as I finished preparing a meal in the tiny kitchen. Even though I wasn't looking directly at her, I was conscious of her gaze on my back, burning into me.

I hadn't said anything much since she'd helped me, and despite my angry-sounding words, my mind kept wandering back to her concerned face. In spite of the fact that she must still be feeling unwell, she hadn't hesitated to jump in and administer first aid. The feel of her hands on mine, pressing down firmly, had been more than pleasant. I imagined them moving from there to my arms, and then snaking them around my waist.

"You moved me," she said, interrupting my restless imagination. "From the car?"

I answered without turning toward her. "Yes."

"How?"

"I carried you."

"Oh."

I smiled and went back to cooking. She was embarrassed.

Imagine if she could read my mind. My smile became a wide grin.

"Will Monato find us here?" she asked. "He followed us before, right?"

"He did. And he could come again," I admitted. "But this is one of *my* places, so he's not as likely to. Besides that, no one knows we're here."

"No one?"

"I really didn't mean that in a sinister way." I met

her eyes.

She didn't look convinced.

"I'll tell you exactly where we are, if you want to know," I said with a sigh.

"You will?" she asked suspiciously.

"Sure. There's no reason not to."

I put a plate of food on her lap, and for a second, she seemed to completely forget about her situation. I handed her a fork, and she took an eager bite.

"Thank you," she said.

"You're welcome."

She was working hard to eat the food slowly, and I watched her with mild amusement, which she pretended not to notice. I couldn't remember the last time I had eaten, either, and I was starving. I took a bite and tried to make conversation, but the pressure of letting her know my plan was making me tenser by the second.

"You were out for four hours," I told her as mildly as I could manage. "Maybe a little more. Definitely not less."

"Okay."

"Thought you'd want to know."

"I was thinking about it."

"*Would* you like to know where we are now, Cass?" I asked.

"Yes," she admitted. "I was thinking about that, too."

I laughed and pulled over one of the chairs from the table. I sat down and watched her face turn serious.

"Those men you were messing with...They're dangerous."

"You said that *you* were dangerous," she reminded me.

"Yes, I did," I agreed.

I tried to look as casual I could, but inside I was shaking a bit at the thought of Monato getting his hands on her.

"Words that come to mind when I think of that…creep," I started.

I had been going to use a stronger descriptor, and I had stopped myself in the name of politeness. As Billy had put it…*Chivalry's not fucking dead.* Not yet, anyway.

"Asshole-ic?" Cass filled in.

"Not too creative," I said a little wryly.

"Lecherous," she offered. "Immoral. Dirtbag. Licentious."

"Better," I agreed with a grin.

"Why did *you* kidnap me?" she asked.

I put my finger on my chin and tapped it thoughtfully.

"I thought you were pretty."

She blushed, and I had to resist a sudden need to run my fingers along her pink-stained cheek.

I was teasing her as way of deflecting her more serious questions. She frowned, took another bite of her stir-fry, and then looked disappointed to realize the food was all gone.

"Sorry there isn't any more," I said. "I'm usually only feeding one person."

"I'm full," she lied.

I raised an eyebrow.

"Don't ever get a job where you have to be anything less than honest," I suggested.

"What do *you* do?" she asked. "I mean besides kidnapping damsels in distress?"

"So you know that you were in distress?" I was half-teasing, half-sincere.

I wanted her to know how dangerous Monato could be, even if I didn't want to give her the details. She examined my face, and seemed to decide I was being serious.

"I assumed that *you* did, too. That's why you came to my rescue in the first place, isn't it?

"I'm not a hero."

I couldn't have her thinking I was. I'm more often in the business of endangering lives than I am in the business of saving them.

"I didn't say you were a hero," she replied slowly.

"And you don't sound surprised by that."

"You kidnapped me," she reminded me once again, and though I hadn't answered her question about what I did for a living, she seemed to have formed an idea. "You could've just…taken out Monato. Or whatever it is you would normally do."

"That's where your mind went? Taking out the enemy?" I smiled again.

"Why is he your enemy?"

"Let's just say his business interferes with mine," I replied evasively, hoping something in my face would tell her not to push too hard with that line of questioning.

"Okay."

I sighed. "He's nothing more than a manipulative scumbag. I don't consider him an enemy. Just a pain in the ass."

"Okay," she said again.

"You know, I could've done something easier than taking him out, too," I suggested. "Like calling the police."

"And...I get the feeling you're not crazy about law enforcement," she stated.

"I'm sure not," I admitted.

"Because you're dangerous, too."

"That's right," I replied, and got up to take our plates over to the sink.

I dropped them in, and steeled myself to steer the conversation toward what I needed—*wanted*—her to do for me.

Chapter Eleven

I couldn't help but follow him with my eyes.

His words should have made me nervous, but they just made me curious. I believed him when he said he was dangerous. But I saw something else, too.

I felt like we were playing a bit of a game, and I didn't know what the prize was. He was tense, and angry, but trying to hide it. I didn't think it was aimed directly at me, but somehow my presence, and our conversation, was making it worse.

John rolled up his sleeves, and I saw that his arms were covered in tattoos. They were intricate. Much more complex than the new one on my back. His had words and symbols and they all swirled together in a beautiful pattern. I wondered automatically how far up they went, and if he had them anywhere else. I looked away, then chastised myself for feeling such a ridiculous mix of emotions.

Maybe that's his problem, too, I thought suddenly, and then brushed it off. *You shouldn't be worried about his feelings. You should be trying to get away.*

I watched him scrub the dishes. His tattoos moved up and down rhythmically as he scrubbed

And you don't really want to get away, do you? I added mentally, and blushed.

"I'm going to need you."

John's abruptness startled me and it didn't help

with my red face—at all.

"For what?" I asked awkwardly.

He sighed loudly. "You've just put me in such an awkward position."

"Not according to Billy," I argued. "I'm just a coincidence."

"So you *were* awake when all that was happening?"

He sounded like he had suspected as much.

"Sort of," I admitted. "At least for a minute or two."

He finished washing up and set the dishes in a drying rack. Then he came back to his chair in front of the couch where I sat. His face was tense.

"The thing is, I can't just let you go," he said, and he seemed almost annoyed by that fact.

"Why not?"

"I can't be totally honest with you, either," he said without answering my question. "Though I wish I could."

His face was completely sincere and open for just a moment, and then went so quickly back to looking irritated that I thought I'd imagined it.

"You've really put me in an awkward position," he repeated.

"I don't think that I did anything, actually," I replied. "I didn't exactly kidnap myself."

I felt a little guilty as soon as the words were out of my mouth. His kidnapping me was just a side effect of his saving me.

"You don't need to keep reminding me." He winced as he said it.

"Let me go," I suggested, and John's eyes

darkened.

He banged his fist on the table suddenly, giving in to whatever frustration he'd been trying to hide. I cringed against the couch.

"Why did you have to jump onto Monato's radar?" he almost-shouted.

"Sorry," I whispered. "I didn't mean to—"

"No. *I'm* sorry," he cut me off in a carefully restrained voice.

He looked like he was trying hard to compose himself again, but his eyes were still blazing.

Dangerous indeed.

"What's the awkward position?" I asked, trying to steer clear of his anger. "Maybe I can help make it...less awkward?"

"I claimed you as mine." John had the grace to sound embarrassed.

As the words came out of his mouth, I had to push down a strange little flutter in my chest.

His.

"And?"

"If I don't follow through, or if I rescind that claim, Monato will move again," he explained. "He's already tried twice, hasn't he?"

He was leaving something out, and I was trying to figure out what it was.

"And he's somehow a more dangerous man than you are?" I pushed.

"To you at least...Much more."

"For how long does he need to think that I'm yours?" I asked.

I blushed as I said it. I thought I must be feeling even more uncomfortable then he was.

"I don't know, exactly," John told me. "Either long enough to make a clean break between us seem plausible, or long enough for him to lose interest. Probably both."

"Then you'll let me go?"

He hesitated for less than a second. "Yes."

"Okay."

"Really? You're just going to go along with what I ask you to do?" He sounded perplexed and relieved.

Almost all of the guarded tension left his body.

That was it? He wanted me to stay?

"Yes," I said firmly, and he relaxed even more.

"Why?"

"Because even if you're not a hero, I do think you saved my life," I admitted. "And I'm not all that interested in finding out what it is Monato's after. He seems…determined."

It was a half-truth, but I didn't want to think about my other reasons for agreeing. Mostly because they directly involved John's mocha-brown eyes.

"Fair enough," he agreed quickly.

"Just tell me what you need," I said.

"First, I'm going to need you to pretend—convincingly—to be my...girlfriend," he told me.

"Why not just say what you actually mean? Be honest. Is *girlfriend* an accurate description of what you need me to be for Monato's sake?" I wanted to know.

He frowned slightly as if surprised I had picked up on something he hadn't meant to give away.

"Listen," I said. "I get that you can't tell me the truth about everything. There's things I don't like to share, too. But don't lie about anything you don't have to lie about, John."

"I like it when you say my name," he told me with a small smile.

"What?" I blushed.

"Just being honest, like you asked."

"Don't be honest about that," I suggested as my face refused to cool down.

"Okay."

"Tell me. What do you *really* need me to pretend to be?" I wanted to know.

I saw the slightest bit of colour in *his* cheeks, and suddenly the tables were turned, and I was holding him captive. He looked away first.

"To Monato, women aren't anything more than a possession," John said. "He won't put any value in my stake on you if you're just my girlfriend. I'm not even sure if it's going to work *this* way."

His voice was tinged with a sudden, dark anger once again, and when he finally met my eyes, I saw it reflected there, too. His body was even tenser than it had been before, and I noticed even though he was keeping very still, he had balled his hands into fists.

So there's something more. A momentary sense of disappointment that it wasn't *just* about me made my heart drop.

"So you need me to be what for you? A possession?"

His eyes burned. "Yes."

"There's something else you're not telling me," I persisted.

"Why are you pushing this?"

"I just want to know what I'm agreeing to," I replied.

"I may have implied to Monato..." he trailed off

and cleared his throat."I'll just show you."

He reached into his pocket and yanked out a ring box. He opened it slowly, and I eyed the ring nervously. It was a stunning piece of jewellery with a red stone set in four delicate claws and surrounded by tiny diamonds. It looked like an antique.

"Is that a ruby?" I asked.

"Yes."

"You've got to be kidding."

"I'm not. Marry me."

I looked into his eyes, and saw something raw there. It made my heart ache to say yes.

But I was *still* missing something.

"John?" I asked, and he seemed to relent.

"The truth is…I'm not exactly giving you a choice here, Cass. Whatever you decide, it won't matter," he sighed, and my illusion of control vanished. "You can agree—as you seem to have done so far—and I will compensate you. Or you can disagree, and then I'll have to keep you here anyway until my own business with Monato is complete and I can find a way to let you go."

So there it was. Or rather…there I was. He'd saved me, only to make me his own prisoner.

"So…be your wife? Or be your hostage?" I asked softly.

He shrugged. "I'll accept the term fiancée."

A flash of annoyance surfaced, and I tried to bury it. His voice was too calm—and it made him seem once again to be exactly what he claimed to be. Dangerous.

"Can I ask some more questions?" I wondered out loud.

"Yes."

"Will you answer them?" I added.

"To the best of my ability."

He waited as I weighed my options. There weren't any. I stared into his face, enjoying the soft patience in his eyes.

"I'll do it," I agreed.

John made a confused face, and he looked almost boyish. I held in a compulsion to reach out and smooth his crinkled brow.

"I thought you had questions," he said.

My face reddened. Anything I had been thinking about asking had gone right out of my head.

"I do. But I'm saving them," I stated.

He accepted my lie with a laugh, then got up and walked into the bedroom. He returned with a slip of paper in his hand. He held it out, and I when took it and read it, I gasped.

"I just addressed it to 'Cass' because I didn't know what last name you wanted," he explained.

"It's Cass Mayer. But it doesn't matter. I can't take this money."

"It's not enough? I'll tack on whatever you lose in wages during your time with me, too…"

"I'm on vacation for another week," I said faintly.

"It'll be a gift, for tax purposes," John added. "No need to share it with the government."

"You're joking, right?"

He had to be joking. It was a check for one hundred, fifty-three thousand dollars—an amount that I would barely make over the next five years. I held the check up. It was embossed with a business emblem—Seever Enterprises—and it looked legitimate. What kind of business John was *really* in, and what made it so dangerous? He didn't look like a thug. His tattoos made him seem a little less than white collar, but I supposed anyone could commit fraud if they were smart enough, and put their mind to it.

But the amount was suspiciously specific. It was an amount that would cover everything I owed and still leave me with exactly an extra twenty grand.

It's really Dean who owes it, I reminded myself.

And then my head snapped up as I leaped to logical conclusion.

"Did you look into my finances?"

"I wouldn't…" he trailed off and sighed. "Yes, I did, a bit."

"Why?"

"Because I needed to know if you were going to be an asset, or a liability," John explained. "And I needed to know what your price would be."

"I don't have a price," I argued. "I'm not a…Wait. That's not what you're really after, is it? Because no amount of money could get me to…"

John was laughing, and I flushed.

"Do you think I'd have to pay for that?" he wanted to know.

"No," I said, but I was suddenly doubtful.

He had said he was dangerous. He was obviously wealthy. And the way he'd discussed me with Monato when we were at the club, and all the talk about women as possessions…He hadn't actually said he'd disagreed with the other man's position on that. I had just made the assumption that he did.

John was suddenly beside me on the couch with one tattooed arm around my shoulders. My heart jumped into my throat as his fingers curled around my upper arm. I tried to swallow, but my mouth was dry. John turned ever so slightly, and used his other hand to tip my chin up. Our faces were so close that I could see every detail of his face.

His eyes were an even deeper shade of brown than I thought. Dark chocolate instead of milk. His eyebrows were thick, and well-shaped, but imperfect. His skin was tanned, and he had a tiny mole right underneath the left side of his full lips. A day or so worth of stubble grazed his cheeks and chin, and I had an urge to reach out and feel it—just to see if it was as rough as it looked.

"Do you think, Cass...that I would have to *pay* for this?" he whispered.

I could feel his breath on my own lips.

No. I tried to say it, but all I could manage was a small gasp.

I shook my head very slightly instead, and John drew his hand from my chin up to my mouth. He traced their shape, and my whole body tingled in response. He ran his fingers along my cheek, up through my hair, and down along my neck.

Then, abruptly, he stopped.

The air around me was hard to draw in, like the wind had been knocked out of me and didn't want to come back. I took a gasping breath.

John stood up and stared down at me.

"I apologize," he said in carefully measured voice. "That was inappropriate. If the amount I've offered you doesn't work, please just let me know, and we can come to another arrangement."

"It's fine," I managed to reply. "I would've done it for nothing."

"I wouldn't have allowed it," he told me coolly.

"Just let me know what you need me to do, and for how long, and I'll do it," I said, trying to sound equally frosty and failing miserably. "But I'll really need to let Blair know I'm not dead."

John's face froze for a second and then he nodded sharply. "I'll bring you a phone."

Chapter Twelve

I didn't want her to make the phone call, and I didn't know why.

Because you don't want to share her, my internal voice acknowledged.

Self-control was clearly going to be a problem. And I was little worried about what she would say to her friend. Billy had told me he'd taken care of it as soon as he'd realized what was going on, but I wasn't convinced. Women don't just let their friends take off with strange men.

I somehow managed to let go of the cell phone without crushing it.

"It's a blocked number," I warned. "And it's a burner phone."

Cass frowned at me. "So?"

I put my hands up. "Just letting you know."

"Anything else I should know?" she asked.

"Just that Billy said he already took care of your friend." I laughed at her sudden look of alarm. "Not like that."

She hesitated. "I'm nervous."

"You're worried about lying to your friend?" I wanted to know. "You think she won't believe you?"

Cass shook her head. "No, not that. Aside from the insanity of the situation, she won't have a reason to doubt me."

"What then?"

She looked away, dialled the phone, and didn't answer. I could tell she knew the talk with her best friend wasn't going to go well. I sat beside her on the couch, pretending it was so I could listen to the extension ring on the other end. But I just wanted to be near her. When she'd implied I was calling her a whore, I'd felt disturbed. Angry. Offended. I'd given her the check to make myself feel better.

What kind of man asks a woman to pretend to be his fiancée? I wondered, and before I could stop, I answered myself. *The same kind of man who pays her to do it.*

Her reaction had made me feel even worse. I'd responded without thinking, set on proving that I had not been insinuating she do anything more than putting on an act. But once I had started, I almost hadn't been able to stop.

"Do you *have* to sit so close to me?" Cass asked.

I grinned. "Yes. I told you. I want to hear what she has to say."

Her friend answered on the fifth ring, sounding sleepy and cranky.

"I got your note" was the first thing she said—so loudly that I had no problem hearing her. "What the fuck?"

"Blair…"

Cass paused, and glanced at me. I *was* sitting close to her for selfish reasons, but now that she had her friend on the phone, I really couldn't take the risk that she was going to give something away. Blair was her best friend, and if I knew anything at all about how women and their best friends work, it was that their radar for things that involved men was almost paranormal.

She's just doing me a favour, I reminded myself, then added, *She's even getting paid for it. That almost makes it legitimate work.*

Her proximity to me kept reminding me all too clearly that I wouldn't mind much at all if it became be something more.

"Billy took care of this," I reminded her in a quiet voice.

"Is that him?" Blair demanded.

"Who?"

"The guy who took you home?"

Cass narrowed her eyes at me, probably wondering what the note had said. I shrugged. I had no idea what Billy had written either.

"What the fuck?" her friend said again. "You went home with a stranger! And now you're staying with him? For how long? And for God's sake. *Why?*"

"Be as honest as you can," I murmured. "It will be easier in the long run."

"He kinda…swept me off my feet," Cass offered lamely.

I rolled my eyes and whispered, "You're a very bad liar. Stick to details that make sense. Stuff she'll believe but doesn't sound crazy."

She rolled her eyes back at me.

"I get it," she muttered.

"What?" said Blair, still so loud that I could hear her.

"I was talking to *him,*" Cass told her.

"You sound annoyed," Blair pointed out. "If he annoys you already, what's it gonna be like in six months?"

I suppressed a grin.

"I'm not going to be here for that long," Cass replied with another questioning glance at me.

I shrugged noncommittally. "Maybe. Maybe not."

"Well how long *are* you going to be there? And where *is* there? And Cass…What the fuck!" Blair yelled.

Cass winced.

"Listen, Blair," she started slowly. "Remember last night when I was upset? And then I went to the bathroom—"

"And didn't come back! And left me a lame-ass note with the waitress!" her friend shouted. "Yeah, it would be hard to forget something like that!"

"Would you please stop hollering at me?" Cass asked.

"Fine!" Blair hollered.

"Thank you," Cass replied with a genuine smile.

"Speak, then," she commanded.

Cass sighed. "Don't freak out, but I think somebody slipped something into my drink."

I nodded and gave her a thumbs up. It was as good a story as any. Blair gasped on the other end of the phone, and Cass started talking again before she could cut in.

"I wasn't feeling well, and this man—the one I'm with now—kind of came to my rescue. I was really out of it, and I just didn't even think. I was scared. He took me out to his car to lie down, and I passed out," she lied.

"What makes you think it wasn't this mysterious stranger who drugged you?" Blair demanded.

"I just know," Cass told her.

"How?"

"He's just...not that kind of guy," she said.

"Oh! He's gay, isn't he?" She sounded both relieved and puzzled.

"No!" Cass protested.

I laughed. With my thigh resting against Cass's leg, there was nothing that could make me more aware of my heterosexuality.

"There's only one other way you could really *know*!"

Cass frowned. "What?"

"You know..." Blair replied. "The same way I know Doug isn't a Doug-ette."

I didn't know what that meant, but Cass's mouth dropped open a little and her face went red.

"It's not like that, either," she said.

"When I told you to get Dean out of your system, that's not what I meant," her friend admonished.

Dean. Jealousy surged, and I pushed it down.

"I said it's not like that," Cass repeated a little more emphatically.

Blair dropped her voice to what I assumed was her approximation of a whisper. "Did he kidnap you? Is he keeping you somewhere against your will? Wait. Is he *listening*?"

I burst out laughing. Who would guess something so outrageous? And the fact that it was very nearly true made me laugh even harder.

"Oh, Blair..." Cass sighed.

"Just so you know, you're not really in love with him," her friend told her, still in that unconvincing whisper. "It's Munchausen syndrome."

"What?" Cass sounded as puzzled as I felt.

"You know. Where you start to feel like you're in love with the person who's holding you hostage," Blair explained.

Cass laughed, even though her cheeks were still an attractive shade of pink. "I think you mean Stockholm syndrome."

"What's that?" her friend asked.

"When a hostage starts to empathize with her captor," Cass said with exaggerate patience.

"Well then what's the other thing?" Blair wanted to know.

"I think that's when someone believes they're sick all the time but they're not," Cass told her.

"Are you sure?"

"Fairly."

"Oh."

There was a brief pause, and I motioned for Cass to hurry it up.

"I'll call you again in a few days," she offered.

"You sound…funny. Okay, but funny," Blair said.

"I'm fine. I'm good. I'll talk to you soon."

Cass hung up and turned to me.

"Was that all right?" she wanted to know.

I grinned, and she ignored my smug expression.

"I need a shower," she said. "And some clothes."

"I can definitely take care of the second part," I told her, and raised an eyebrow. "But I think we'll need to know each other a bit better before I help you out with the first part."

"You're enjoying this more than you should be," she told me, then stomped off to the bathroom.

I watched her go. It was true. I *was* enjoying her

company. But I still wasn't looking at all forward to dragging her into my world.

"There's some spare sweats and a T-shirt under the sink in there," I called after her.

"Whatever," she snapped, and I grinned.

The second she closed the bathroom door, I went out into the hall and dialled Billy.

"Thought better of your situation?" he asked without bothering with a greeting.

I gritted my teeth. I didn't want to tell him that I had gone on to complicate my situation even more. "No."

"Too bad," Billy sighed. "You ready to apologize?"

"No."

"Oh, you dump my ass unceremoniously on the side of the road, and let me guess—now you *need* me?" he asked.

"This isn't the type of relationship where I have to apologize to you," I snapped.

"I'm aware of how things work," Billy replied, ignoring my tone. "But it never hurts to ask."

"I'm supposed to have a meeting with someone in twenty minutes," I said. "We're at the Empress. How far away are you?"

"Five minutes," he replied without hesitating, and I decided he had likely been tracking me anyway. "On my way."

Chapter Thirteen

I let the water run into the bathtub for a few minutes before stepping under the hot stream. Standing up had made me dizzy, and I wanted some time to make sure I wasn't going to fall over and crack my head. I hadn't wanted to admit my momentary wooziness to John, either. I was worried he would either refuse to let me shower at all, or worse, *actually* try to help me bathe. He'd already warned me that if I wasn't out in twenty minutes, he was coming in after me.

Like the rest of the place, the bathroom was hotel-like. It had an extra-long countertop and plain white fixtures. The towels were thick and fluffy, and white too. But when I glanced into the tub, I saw that there was a nearly full bottle of salon shampoo, and some nice conditioner as well.

I peeled off the jeans I had borrowed from Blair, then lifted off the sleeveless top, too. I winced a little as it rubbed against the covered-up but still-fresh tattoo. What had Yun said about getting it wet? Was it to wait twenty-four hours? Or forty-eight? I'd take my chances. I'd try not to soak it, but I needed to get clean. In fact, I had probably never needed it so badly.

With my back turned carefully away, I scrubbed my hair twice, then let the hot water rinse away the stink of the club and the lingering scent of ether.

I shivered again when I thought about that. Even

though I didn't want to dwell on what it was Monato had been intending to do with me, I couldn't stop my mind from wandering there. I once again considered that in spite of his claims otherwise, John probably really *had* saved my life.

His deep brown eyes jumped to the front of mind, and I immediately tried to steer my thoughts away. I was rather proud of the way I was holding up. In spite of the world swimming around me, I hadn't actually puked when I'd jumped up to tend to his cut. And even though I was still a bit nauseous, I had managed to eat. And then I'd started to feel a little more whole.

Did John live in the room full-time? I'd been unconscious when he'd brought me in and I instantly coloured at the realization that he must have carried me up in his very capable arms. I forcibly refocused my thoughts.

I could only base my opinions of John's living situation on what I had and hadn't seen. I hadn't spied a suitcase, or anything else that indicated a short-term stay. But I didn't think there were a ton of hotels in the city that rented long-term. We clearly weren't somewhere fancy, but it wasn't a roach motel either. I had noted a window, but no balcony. There was an ashtray on the table. I hadn't seen John smoke at all though, so maybe it was just for if Billy stopped by. And a lot of hotels didn't allow smoking inside at all. Then again, they were probably both in the habit of doing what they wanted, where they wanted.

And there was John's comment about me not being able to use the gun even if I could get to it...Did I seem like that much of a wimp?

Maybe, I admitted to myself as I massaged in some

of the pleasantly scented conditioner.

After all, I *had* resolved not to say anything except in response to direct questions, then asked a dozen of my own. Why was John putting up with my questions anyway?

A knock on the door let me know I had used up my allotted bathroom time. I rinsed quickly, then turned off the water and grabbed a towel. I eyed my clothes. I wasn't looking forward to putting them back on. The alternative was the clothes John had offered to lend me. I sighed and peeked into the cupboard. They were there, folded and waiting. I grabbed them and dressed quickly before I could change my mind. They were ridiculously big, of course, but at least they were clean. I wondered who did John's laundry. I couldn't imagine this was the kind of place that had a service. Maybe a laundromat? I smiled at the thought of the six foot five, tattooed man sticking quarters in the machine while the other launderers watched in awe.

The knock came on the door again, and I ran my fingers through my hair before I opened the door.

"You look the part already," said a gruff voice.

Billy.

"I thought you weren't sticking around for this," I said, trying to sound confident.

He laughed. He was younger than I had first imagined, but still looked quite a bit older than John. He was much shorter than John, too, and stockier. A puckered scar marked one of his cheeks, and it was a little bit frightening. Even though he was smiling, I detected something else in his eyes. It made me nervous.

"The impending car chase influenced my

decision," he told me.

"Uh huh."

"I would've changed my mind, anyway, once John told me his plan," Billy informed me. "It seemed a little—no wait, completely—bat-shit crazy, so of course I had to check it out."

"Hoping he'll fail?" I asked.

"Oh, you're sharp, aren't you?"

Where is John, anyway? The question came to me a little belatedly.

Billy followed my anxious gaze, but didn't comment. There was something about the man that rubbed me the wrong way.

"And it just so happens that not everyone is as comfortable with risk as our mutual friend," he told me.

I didn't answer, and he pointed to a suitcase on the couch.

"Clothes," he stated. "Hope they fit better than John's do. Or maybe I don't hope that, but I'm sure it will turn out to be true."

He eyed me appreciatively and I realized a little too late that I had forgotten to put on my bra underneath the oversized T-shirt. I crossed my arms protectively across my chest, but refused to take the bait.

"You wanna watch some TV?" Billy asked.

"No."

"You wanna sit and stare at each other instead?"

"God, no."

The older man got up and walked over to flick on the television set.

"Why are you here?" I wanted to know.

"To keep you safe," he replied.

"You mean to make sure I won't run off?"

He snorted, and I wasn't sure whether or not to be insulted.

"John asked me to come," he elaborated. "And I might not be crazy about his idea here—hell, I'm not even thrilled he rescued you in the first place—but it's not my job to question his decisions."

"What *is* your job?" I asked.

"To go where John tells me to. To keep his ass safe. And apparently to be a personal shopper for every girl he picks up," Billy told me irritably.

"Does he pick up a lot of girls?" I asked before I could help myself.

"None."

He turned up the TV, and that was my cue to shut my mouth.

Chapter Fourteen

I had to force myself to stop tapping my fingers on the dash. I was on time for my scheduled meeting. Five minutes early, even. But I wasn't in the mood to wait.

"Control your tells, Seever," I muttered to myself as I realized my fingers were banging away again.

The thing is, I'm busy almost all the time. I directly employ—if it can be called that—about ten guys with regularity, and probably closer to twenty if you count the mercenaries. Though I prefer not to count them, if I can avoid it. Twenty doesn't sound like a lot. But there's other factors at play. For starters, I don't trust any of them completely, other than Billy. A few I can just barely have enough faith in to get a job done. The majority I can't even count on for that. So there's a lot of micromanaging. There's a lot of telling people things on a need-to-know basis. Of course, there's a lot of me just doing things because I don't think anybody else is going to do it right.

And none of that is a problem.

The less time I have to rest, the less time I have to sit and think about what drives me, and the less time I have to think about what turned me from a regular guy into this hulking criminal mastermind.

And no time to wonder what's going to happen when I've achieved my goal. I tried to keep my fingers still.

Truthfully, Cass was the very first thing to distract me from my job, and from my little obsession. There was just something about her. I liked her frank honesty and her direct questions. I liked *her*. Period.

A small knock on the car window startled me so badly that I actually jumped, and then burst out laughing. A twelve-year-old-ish kid was standing outside my car, and regarding me with uncertainty. I rolled the window down

"Mr. Seever?" he said.

"That's me," I agreed with a grin.

"My associate is waiting for you. He wants you to get out and follow me," the kid told me.

"Does he now?" I let my smile slip as my business-side took over automatically.

The kid nodded.

"I suppose he wants me to leave my weapons behind, too?" I asked.

He nodded again.

"And what did he tell you to do to me if I didn't comply?"

"He actually kind of assumed you wouldn't," said a deeper voice.

The kid backed off, and I recognized the speaker from Yun's description. The tall, thin man tossed back his shaggy hair, put his hand on the kid's shoulder, and nodded at me.

"Hello," I said.

"Seever," he greeted. "I'm Vance. My boss sent me to answer your questions. And you can keep your gun if it means that much to you."

I shrugged. "I didn't bring it, actually."

"Let's talk," he suggested. "The boss said that Yun

was rather vague about your needs."

"Get in," I replied.

"Get into your car? Where you *don't* have a gun?" Vance didn't exactly sound disbelieving—just indifferent.

But his eyes were calculating. He came around and let himself in.

"My boss did mention you were after some specific ink. But it looks like you've already got a preferred artist," he said as he eyed my arms.

"I *am* after some specific ink. But it's not for me," I replied.

"And you've got something to show me?" he asked.

"I might," I answered.

He sighed. "You've gone to a lot of trouble to find us. Close to ten tattoo parlours from what my boss told me. Are you going to play shy now?"

I handed him the drawing of the tattoo and he surveyed it coolly. I had debated what to show him, and what to tell him. It was true, I had spent a long time trying to find this connection. I'm not in the habit of showing all of my cards at the beginning of a game, but I wanted it to be done. I was getting impatient with it all.

Finally, said a small, relieved voice in my head, and I pushed it aside.

"You know this design?" I wanted to know.

"Where did you get this?"

"My brother."

I didn't elaborate. I was pretty sure Yun had probably shared everything with him anyway.

"You want to stay away from this," Vance said.

"I guess I'll take that as a yes."

"My boss was wrong. I don't have the information you want," he told me.

"How do you know what information I want?" I replied.

"The man who commissioned this particular tattoo did so over the phone."

I let my impatience show as I snapped, "I'm aware. Our mutual friend, Yun, already told me."

Vance ignored my irritation. "He wanted a way to mark his women as his property. I refused on behalf of my boss. Even *we* have certain standards. I then received a personal visit from the man's friend—he came to convince me I'd made a bad decision."

He rolled up his right sleeve and exposed a trail of cigarette burns. But I was distracted.

His women.

My mind went to Monato instantly, and then to Cass, draped lifelessly across his back. Was he involved? It seemed like too much of a coincidence to point to anything but Monato's culpability. I balled my hands into fists, and nearly missed the next part of Vance's story.

"His friend also brought the first girl in, and I did my best to replicate his over-the-phone description," Vance went on. "My first attempt, the man deemed a failure. He sent his friend back to let me know."

The man rolled his sleeve up further, and I saw four jaggedly healed knife wounds.

"I'd be curious to know who your brother is, and how *he* got the drawing," he told me. "It's the one I made so the client wouldn't feel a need to punish any more of my mistakes."

"If you can't help me, that's fine," I replied as I ignored his mildly curious look.

"I don't think of myself as a criminal," Vance said. "I'm an artist."

"I don't care what you think you are. I don't even care what you actually are," I told him.

"But I think you do care," he stated. "And I must admit…I'm wondering why."

"Because *I'm* a criminal?" I asked.

He nodded once.

"You didn't like it when the man who commissioned these tattoos wanted you to brand his women, and I don't blame you." I met his eyes as I spoke. "But what would you do if you thought he killed that little brother of yours?"

Vance's eyes snapped up, truly expressive for the first time, and it was my turn to nod.

"So you might understand my motivation, at least a little bit," I said.

"I did these tattoos against my better judgement," he admitted. "But I don't know your brother. How exactly did he die?"

"Unpleasantly," I replied.

"He had this drawing on him when he died," Vance surmised.

"Yes."

"Tattooing people under the influence is how I've made a living for the last twelve years, but aside from these women, they've all been at their own request."

"Could you identify the man who commissioned the ink?" I asked.

Vance hesitated. "He isn't a pleasant man, Mr. Seever. And I don't know his name. Perhaps my boss might not even know it. And even if we did, I probably wouldn't be permitted to share it."

"I wouldn't ask you to," I told him.

"You would ask, if you really thought I knew. And if it meant finding the man who killed your brother."

"Yes, in that case I probably would," I admitted. "Could you describe the man who brought the girls in?""

Vance was quiet, looking over my shoulder. He met my eyes and shook his head.

"No."

I knew instantly that he was lying.

I gritted my teeth. "You can't? Or you won't?"

"I can't," he said emphatically.

He was lying again. I narrowed my eyes and looked carefully at the other man. His deception was too obvious to have been an accident. He saw me realize it and gave me an almost imperceptible nod. He heaved the car door open violently.

"I have no reason to tell you what you want to know!" he shouted as he climbed out.

"Hey!"

It was then that I spotted the truck cruising around the corner. It circled once, then it stopped, just up the road. A big guy in a suit stepped out and leaned too casually against the door. I immediately realized the reason for Vance's little display. I watched in frustration as he disappeared up the block. I was sure he had been about to give me something more but my hands were tied by my own weakness. I watched helplessly as the man in the suit climbed back into the truck, and cursed my morality. I couldn't pursue him without endangering Vance's life.

I tapped the dashboard, and worked at not slamming my fist into the windshield.

"Godammit," I muttered.

A phone rang from somewhere in the passenger side door. I reached down, surprised to find a cheap, plastic cell buried in the compartment there. It rang again and I flipped it open.

"Mr. Seever," Vance said, impassive once more. "Do not say my name."

"All right."

He hesitated for a moment, then spoke slowly. "I have a habit of not drawing conclusions or asking questions that don't relate directly to my art. In my line of business, I'm sure you can understand why. And I don't blame you for pursuing the man who killed your brother, presuming it *is* the same one…"

"But?"

"Sometimes it's better to just let things be. If you can't change the past, find a way to move on."

Cass…Her soft skin and sweet smile. Was she a step forward?

I pushed down the sudden rush of emotion.

"Not an option," I growled.

"The man who brought these girls to me was just an idiot with a gun," Vance added. "Lethal, but stupid."

"Would you let it go?" I asked,

"No."

I waited.

"I may be able to do something better than providing a description of the man who brought the girls in," he said after a brief pause. "I have him recorded on video surveillance. When I've cleared it with my boss, I'll send a still image to this phone, so keep it handy."

He hung up, and white-hot satisfaction surged through my body. My hunt was almost over.

I drove back the long way, partly because I wanted to disguise my whereabouts—just because the truck hadn't followed me didn't mean I needed to make myself a target. But it was mostly because I wanted to sort out my thoughts. And they weren't pleasant ones.

I *wanted* it to be Monato who had commissioned the tattoos. And if it *was* him, and he had also killed my brother…

Anger crashed through me at the thought that the little creep had been involved in Colin's death. For several seconds it almost crippled me. Everything about him had always set my teeth on edge. At least I would be able to fully justify my hatred for him.

My body tensed up again, and I breathed carefully in through my nose, trying to calm myself. I'd deal with him as soon as I found out if he was responsible, and as soon as the opportunity allowed it.

As I finally arrived at my home-of-the-moment and parked my car, I knew I was going to have to be patient. And when the photo did come through to the phone, I would likely have to wait until after I'd made sure Cass was safe before making a decision about what to do.

I let myself into the building with a nod at the security guard, then made my way up to the room. My mood was lightening. I paused outside the door, and buried a smile. I realized that I was looking forward to seeing how Cass had dealt with Billy.

"Hey," I said as I went in.

Billy was watching football, and Cass was sleeping on the couch beside him, slumped purposely away.

"You all right?" Billy asked me.

"Fine."

"Then why are you grinning like an idiot?"

"I had some bad news," I told him.

"This makes you happy?" Bill shook his head.

"No."

He waited.

I glanced down at Cass. Her hair was shiny and clean, and she was wearing my clothes.

"I get it," Billy said. "She's pretty."

"She's more than pretty." The words were out before I could stop them.

"I have *never* said this to you before," Billy told me. "But, John. You are in over your head."

"She's just a girl," I lied.

Billy leaned over casually and stroked Cass's arm. She sighed contentedly and my fist closed involuntarily.

"Enough," I said sharply. "If she's supposed to be my wife-to-be, I can't have you touching her like that."

Billy's eyebrows shot up. "Your wife-to-be?"

"Yes."

He looked down at Cass's left hand, and I saw surprise register on his face when he realized the ring was there.

Billy put his hands up defensively. "It's your game."

"It's not a game. Lives are at risk."

"Jesus, you're sensitive today," Billy said. "The girl is rubbing off on you, isn't she?"

He was watching me carefully. He stood up and stretched and gave Cass a slow once over.

"I'm not bloody kidding," I hissed. "Keep your eyes off her."

"So now it's my hands *and* my eyes?" Billy asked mockingly without looking away from Cass.

I stalked over to the older man and grabbed him by the collar.

"Just a girl?" he wondered out loud. "Care to amend that?"

"It's okay." Cass's nervous voice cut through the tension. "Take it easy, John."

I turned to look at her, and I exhaled slowly as I let Billy go. The older man was just watching me with deep scowl on his face.

"If you don't control that right away, this isn't going to work," he observed.

It dawned on me that Billy was being deliberately antagonistic.

He was testing me to prove a point, and I had probably failed.

I nodded curtly and turned my back to him.

"Fine," I muttered. "Let's just get this show on the road."

Chapter Fifteen

When Billy finally left us alone again, I eyed the suitcase skeptically. I wasn't sure what to expect, but I was pretty sure the older man and I would have different tastes.

"It'll all be designer," John told me. "And appropriate for the…game, as Billy called it."

"Does he work for you?" I asked.

"Did he say he did?"

"He implied that he was your errand boy."

"You could say that," John replied with a laugh. "And I'm sure Billy would see it that way. Though I've always assumed he thinks of himself as my keeper."

He'd cracked open a ginger ale and was visibly more relaxed with the bottle in his hand, and the other man gone.

"Ginger ale?" I asked with a smile.

"I think Billy would agree that alcohol has influenced my decisions quite enough over the past twenty-four hours," John replied wryly.

"I don't like him," I said.

It wasn't exactly true. But there was something about the man that made me question his motivations. And I still didn't know what to make of the bit of the exchange I saw when I woke up.

"He's not so bad. I trust him. And he gets the job done," John told me.

I unzipped the suitcase and peered inside. It looked like an awful lot of black lace. I pawed through it, trying to find something I'd be willing to wear. I was sorely disappointed.

"I can't wear these," I said as I held up a pair of black pants.

They were shimmery and held together at the sides by long ties that went from the hip to the ankle.

"Or this," I added, and yanked out a long-sleeved top.

It was so dark purple that it looked black, too, but it was sheer pretty much everywhere but the chest.

"Then that's what I think you *should* wear," John stated.

"Seriously? Why?"

He took another big swig of his soda. "Because you're going to have to be the opposite of the girl you usually are."

"You don't know what kind of girl I am," I countered.

"Cass not-Sternlight. Only child, parents deceased. Straight A student in both high school and college. Excellent credit. At least until a year or so ago," John said.

"Congrats," I replied. "You successfully stalked me on the web."

"You really don't keep as much online as most people," he said. "I had to dig."

"I like to keep a low profile," I stated lightly.

He leaned forward and reached me effortlessly with one of his long arms. He pulled me so I was facing him. I met his eyes because I had to.

"You're smart," he told me. "Quiet. Conservative.

A hard worker. You do a job that brings a lot of personal satisfaction, but little pay. Haven't quite figured out what, but it involves children. Your heart was badly broken, so you've built a wall around it to ensure it won't happen again..."

"That's enough," I said, even although he was already trailing off.

Tears formed in my eyes, and I willed them to stop. I didn't want him—or anyone—to know so many personal things about me just from looking at my face. John's hands were still on my arms, and I could feel them through the thin fabric of my borrowed T-shirt. His face was serious, and his eyes were full of understanding.

I leaned away, and when John let me go, I felt the sudden loss of contact with a disturbing acuteness.

"I'm smart, too, Cass," he informed me. "And very observant. In my business, it pays to be able to read people."

"So what? You want me to be an outgoing dummy, with no education, two living parents, a crappy job, and to have an unbroken heart? What happened to keeping as close to the truth as possible?"

John took a slow sip of his ginger ale before answering. "That was for people who already know you. For my purposes, I do want you to be smart, but street smart. I need you to not care about what you do, if you do anything at all. Your parents are irrelevant. You don't need an unbroken heart. You need no heart at all. Be a bitch."

"You make it sound so appealing," I replied.

"I need to make this work, Cass," he told me in a softer voice.

"Because lives are at risk?" I asked.

He nodded.

"Whose?" I wanted to know.

"Mine, always. And now yours." John hesitated. "I'm a dangerous man. I've said it before, and I'll say it again. But Monato is…something else. This business arrangement between you and I has the benefit of offering you some protection against him. If you chose to leave—if you didn't want to go along with our deal, I couldn't guarantee you anything."

My heart quickened at the sincerity in his voice.

"I thought you said I *couldn't* leave," I reminded him.

"I would do everything in my power to stop you from going," he admitted. "But if there was some reason I couldn't stop you, or if things got out of control…And if something happened as a result, I would consider myself responsible. I don't know if I could live with that."

I shivered. "Why bother to pay me then? Why not just offer me protection in exchange for our arrangement?"

"When all is said and done, and I'm through with Monato, I'll need something else from you. Your silence," he told me too casually.

The way he said the words *through with* made me nervous.

"You can still back out," he offered.

"But then you wouldn't be able to guarantee my safety, even if you kept me here against my will," I stated.

"No." John looked at his hands. "And I don't believe in unnecessary casualties."

"I'll put this on," I told him, and held up the horrifying pants and see-through top.

John's face flooded with relief, then he covered it with a grin. I started to make my way to the bathroom to get changed, but John grabbed my arm gently.

"What?" I said, trying to ignore the way his touch made me feel.

"It's five in the morning, and I've been awake for something close to seventy hours," he said. "If you don't mind, I'd like to get some sleep."

"Fine. Be lazy," I teased.

I hadn't thought about the time at all. John had left the lights off for my benefit, and the shades were still drawn.

"Not all of us took a nap," he replied with a raised eyebrow.

"And you trust me to not run off the second you're asleep?" I wondered out loud.

"I do, Cass," he said. "And even if I didn't…Someone would stop you before you got far."

I felt the tingle of apprehension again, but John just laughed.

"This time, I'll take the couch," he told me

He placed the suitcase on the table then flopped down. He covered himself with the blanket I'd been using, and promptly fell asleep, leaving me feeling a little bit lost.

I wandered into the bedroom, wondering if I'd be able to sleep again so soon.

It wasn't much different than I'd pictured it. It had one bed instead of two, and there was a print of a tree rather than the ocean, but aside from that it was pretty plain. The bed was made, and I immediately doubted

John actually slept in it. I just couldn't imagine him, with his bold tattoos and intimidating physique, curled up under the rose-covered comforter.

The hotel doesn't seem like his style at all, I mused, and blushed as though he could hear my presumptuous thought from the other room. Two or three conversations didn't mean I knew anything about the man's tastes.

I folded the clothes I'd taken out of the suitcase and placed them on the nightstand. I set the ridiculous check on top, and told myself I'd never actually ever cash it. I felt both a tiny glimmer of hope and a huge stab of guilt when I imagined myself walking into the bank with it. It would probably be the cause for quite a bit of discussion.

Would I really *not be expected to pay taxes on it?* I doubted it. *How would I explain what it was for? Nobody just gave a gift like that to a near stranger.*

But with that amount of money, I'd be able to pay off every red cent Dean had racked up in my name. I might be able to afford a better apartment, and I wouldn't have to live on instant noodles and canned orange juice anymore. My income would finally be my own.

I peeled back the flowered blanket and crawled into the bed, imagining what that would be like.

I couldn't do it.

Before I met Dean, I hadn't had any money, but I hadn't had any real debt, either. I had my part time job, and even though it was mostly in a trust, I'd had the inheritance from my parents to keep me going. Then Dean proposed.

"Cass," he said. "I don't want my wife to be

slumming it in the Java Bean."

I looked up in surprise and then I answered as if he had simply misspoken.

"It's not exactly slumming it, Dean," I laughed with a red face. "The Java Bean is in an office building full of lawyers and doctors and a giant bank."

Dean watched me carefully as he replied. "Yes. Which is well and good for someone who needs a second income. But my *wife* won't need that."

Then I got it. I was stunned, actually. We were taking it slow, as was my style. In a year and a half we never talked about moving in together. I never met his parents, who always seemed to be in Europe. Marriage hadn't even crossed my mind. I was only seventeen.

"Well?" Dean prodded.

"Yes," I gulped. "Okay."

"Not right away," he assured me. "I'm not in a hurry, and I don't think you are, either."

Then came my moment of weakness.

You know everything about him, said a small, reasonable-sounding voice in my head. *Where he works, what he makes, what he eats for dinner. You know his habits and his hang-ups. You know exactly what to expect when you're with him.*

I believed at the time that Dean and I were alike in all the right ways, and different in all the right ways, too. He had few friends, like me, and preferred it that way. He was adventurous, and I wasn't, but it gave me the opportunity to try a lot of new things I would never have even considered otherwise. We balanced each other out.

Our relationship wasn't perfect, and I was glad about that, too. Because the little imperfections are what keep things real.

You're right, I replied to the small voice. *This is it.*

"Why wait? I'll be eighteen in three months. Let's do it then," I said to Dean, and he grinned.

So ninety-one days later, we recited the vows in front of a judge, and started saving to buy a house. Or at least that's where he told me my money was going. I handed over my inheritance and my pay checks so he could invest them.

"We're fine," he told me easily. "We'll scrimp for a while, but we'll be laughing when we can buy the two storey with the white picket fence while everyone else is still living in their boxy apartments."

Only Dean hadn't saved a penny. And when he ran out of cash, he'd borrowed under my name. There had been gambling debt, and botched business ventures and—

I cut myself off, mid-memory, forcing myself back to the present.

I pulled the flowered blanket from John's bed up to my chin and stared across the room to where I'd left the check. Even in the dark, I could see it sitting there.

I deserved a break. I truly did.

But I still wasn't sure if I'd take it.

I drifted off, dreaming of balance free credit cards and apartment buildings that didn't smell like mothballs.

Chapter Sixteen

"It's not so bad," I said.

Cass snorted, but her smile was genuine, like she was secretly rather pleased with the outcome. She smoothed her hair a little self-consciously.

"You look good," I added.

"I look like a cheap club rat," she replied, but she was smiling.

I pretended to survey her outfit again. The pants were cinched up tightly along the ribboned seams, and no part of her leg was actually exposed. The top was not nearly as sheer as it had looked when she held it up in the room. It hinted at bare skin rather than showing it all off. The affect was enticing. She'd grabbed a long-sleeved, bomber length velvet jacket from the suitcase, and with her heeled boots, she was anything but cheap.

"You're too classy to be a club rat." The sincerity in my voice was obvious.

She gave me a slow once over. I'd showered and shaved, and I was dressed in a fitted black T-shirt and dark-wash jeans. I'd thrown on a gray sports coat, too. I enjoyed the feel of her eyes on me, and smiled at the clear appreciation reflected on her face.

Her cheeks coloured as she realized I was watching her examine me.

"I wish I had some mascara," she told me with an embarrassed laugh. "And some hairspray."

"I'm glad you don't have either," I replied.

I placed my hands under the collar of her jacket and pulled her hair out so it hung midway down her back. My fingers paused very briefly on her neck as I shook it all out, and my body heated up in response to the feel of her soft skin. She cleared her throat and took a quick step away.

"You're going to have to get over your aversion to being touched by me if this is going to work," I teased.

"I don't mind…" she stopped herself, and I grinned as I realized what she had been going to say.

I don't mind being touched by you.

"I'll work on it," she said instead.

"Pretend you like it," I suggested.

I threaded my fingers through hers. My hand instantly got warm, and it was easy for me to admit—at least to myself—that if anything, *I* liked this a little too much.

I hadn't slept well, and as good as it felt holding onto Cass, I was uncharacteristically nervous about what we were about to do. Not that I minded lying to my associates—dishonesty was an integral part of my business—but it was the first time I included someone else. And because it was *her*, I was doubly apprehensive.

"Where are we going?" Cass had asked over our bacon and eggs breakfast.

"It's just an experiment," I replied. "To test out our plan. Don't worry. These are some of my most trusted clients. I just want to see how they react to you. And I want to start some rumours."

"Rumours?"

I shrugged. "I can't think of a better way to solidify

my claim on you. Then I can still conduct a little business."

"What kind of business is it you're in?"

I blinked at her. I half-expected her to balk at my use of the word *claim*. It hadn't occurred to me that she'd ask about my work directly. It threw me off. She looked at me expectantly, and I found myself speaking without thinking.

"It's complicated. I'm chasing down a…" I trailed off as I realized I'd been about to tell her everything. "I'm in finance."

I was sure she caught my quick correction, but she'd just taken another sip of her coffee and let it go.

I squeezed her hand as we waited for the elevator, and the warmth travelled up my arm. She tried to pull away, but I made her hang on.

The elevator dinged and the doors opened. We stepped inside, and I was suddenly aware of how very small the space was. Her leg accidentally rubbed against mine, and I drew in slow breath.

"You nervous?" I asked, trying to fill the air with something other than tension. "These guys won't be so bad."

She turned and looked up at my face, and I felt lightheaded. She must've felt it, too, because when I touched her face, she stumbled into me. I grabbed her gently and righted her. I cupped her chin with my palm.

"Cass? Are you okay?"

She shook her head, then changed it to a nod.

"I'm okay."

"Did you hear what I said before about it not being so bad?" I asked.

"Sorry, I think I spaced out. Must still be the

aftereffects of the ether," she told me.

I let my hand fall away from her face. She grabbed it and rethreaded her fingers through mine. My heart beat a little faster, but it didn't stop me from worrying.

"We should go back," I said, not bothering hide my concern. "I pushed you too soon."

"No, I'm fine."

I felt doubtful, but as the elevator came to a stop, and I let go of her hand, she took a deep breath and smiled. We stepped out into the lobby. It was completely empty. There wasn't even a concierge at the desk.

"John, are you the only one who lives here?"

"It's my building. I'm overseeing the renovation," I replied. "No one lives here right now except my security team. That's why I knew it was a safe place to bring you."

"So…you're in real estate, too?" she asked.

"Sometimes."

I pulled her through the lobby and then outside. I could tell from her face that she still couldn't fathom where we were. The front of the hotel was covered with scaffolding and blue-tinged plastic. Ten foot hedges surrounded the property, and all we could see was green. There weren't any other buildings within our view, and we weren't within the city limits.

A vehicle pulled up, and Cass's eyes widened a little at the sight of it. It was an impressive one, and I'd had it brought around on purpose. It was a boat of a car—red with a black soft top roof, and huge seats. It also happened to be my favourite. A perfectly restored, 1964 Pontiac Parisienne with custom paint.

"Go big, or go home," I murmured.

The man who stepped out of it was big, too. He was about six feet tall, and had a chest like a barrel. He flicked his eyes in Cass's direction for just a moment before he handed the keys over to me.

"Are you all right, boss?" he asked.

I glared at him, but I cringed inwardly at the side of me Cass was about to see.

Might as well get it over with.

"Boss?"

"What are you suggesting, Yuri?" I replied coldly.

I pretended not to notice Cass's visible surprise at my tone. I made myself smirk, and I was aware that there was something cruel about my expression. Men bigger than Yuri had backed away from it.

"Do you really think I can't handle this little girl?" I added derisively.

Cass opened her mouth, then closed it. Yuri looked downright terrified.

"No, sir," he managed in a somewhat clear voice.

"Are you sure about that?" I asked.

"Yes, sir."

I took a step closer to him. "You'd better be. Now open the door for the lady."

Yuri rushed to the other side of the car, and Cass followed him, looking uncomfortable. She didn't meet his eyes—or mine—as she climbed in and buckled up. I climbed in, too, and started the car without a word. I slammed on the gas. We whipped down the winding driveway which led up to the hotel, and cut quickly onto the highway.

After a few minutes, I cleared my throat.

"Cass…" he started. "I should've warned you about that."

"Do you have multiple personalities, or what?" she blurted out.

I threw back my head and laughed. "That's just about the most apt, honest question I've been asked in God knows how long."

She frowned. "What?"

I laughed again. "Never mind. I'm sorry."

"Okay," she said uncertainly.

She clearly wanted more of an explanation.

I shifted gears and sped up. Cass looked out the window, and I wondered if she realized where we were—miles outside the city on the highway that led through the countryside and eventually wound down into an old industrial area. She looked annoyed

"All right," I sighed. "Are you going to make me admit it?"

"Admit what?"

"I have a reputation to uphold," I told her. "I can't do what I do, and be overtly kind at the same time."

"So…You were *faking* that meanness back there?" she wanted to know.

"Not exactly. I'm really that guy more often than I am this one," I admitted.

"This guy seems better," she said.

"It's been a nice change for me, too. But I hate Yuri, and he hates me. He's a mercenary. He'll do anything he's paid to do. And sometimes I need that. Which makes me hate him even more," I explained.

"And why does Yuri hate you, then?" she wondered out loud.

"Because I'm the one with the money."

"Couldn't you just use someone else? Aren't there any mercenaries out there who you do like?" she asked.

"No."

"I'm not sure I understand. You hate him because he breaks the law for money. No offence, but there seems to be a bit of irony there," she observed.

Her face coloured as she realized she had just called me a criminal.

I shrugged it off. "It's a family business for me. There's honour in that."

Cass frowned and pursed her lips, looking like she had her doubts. I waited but she didn't voice them.

"I can tell by your expression that you don't agree," I stated, and it was her turn to shrug.

"I guess we'll have to agree to disagree."

"Let me ask *you* something."

"Go ahead," she said.

"Other than my 'meanness,' does none of this bother you?" I wanted to know.

"Bother me how?"

"Yesterday, you were going about your daily life, worrying about whether to go to yoga or zumba—or whatever it is you normally do on Thursdays. Today you're a kidnap victim, pretending to be a thug's fiancée so you can avoid being killed by another thug," I said.

"I'm trying not to think of you as a thug," she replied lightly. "Although with that little show back there…"

"It's as true a description as any, though," I insisted. "And in just a minute, you might not be able to think of me as anything else."

We slowed down, and I pulled the car into a gated industrial park. I stopped in front of the fence and glanced at the camera on top of barbed wire. The red light flashed an acknowledgment, and I grinned up at it—the same smirk I'd given Yuri. After a moment, the gate slid open automatically. We cruised slowly into the lot, weaving carefully between structures. We halted at a large building with blacked out windows.

"This is it," I announced, and I hoped she knew that I meant the beginning of our experiment as well as arrival at our destination.

A man who could've been Yuri's twin rushed out of the building, and waited at attention beside the car. The second I turned the engine off, the big man opened my door. When we were both out, I handed him the keys without speaking and took Cass's hand.

"I'm going to give her a little tour of *my* warehouse, all right?" I said to the big guard, who nodded.

It was partly my need to stall the inevitable, and partly a sudden urge to show off that prompted me to make the spontaneous decision.

I continued to hold Cass's hand, and pulled her past the first few buildings to a huge one. It always reminded me of an airplane hangar, and I grinned at Cass's openly awed face.

"C'mon," I urged.

She followed me in, and I was pleased to see her jaw drop as she took in my collection.

"Are you, like, *really* rich?" she asked, and turned a furious shade of red.

Was she always so easily embarrassed? I hoped immediately it was just *me* who made her blush like that. I desperately wanted to be the only one who affected her this way.

"Not *really really*," I replied with an exaggerated

wink. "I just like bikes."

"Apparently," Cass observed dryly.

It was true. The building clearly displayed my passion.

For me, one of the hardest parts of the business was learning to spend money like it was nothing. I could happily and easily rob a competitor blind, but each extravagance—the expensive clothes, the overpriced cars, and even my trendy apartment—was a forced one. One of the quirks of growing up poor, I think.

My mom had passed away when Colin was just a baby, and even though I had vague memories of taking trips, and of riding in a nice car, most of my childhood had been spent scrimping and saving on my dad's low-level salary. The sudden windfall at eighteen—the inheritance my mom left for both Colin and me—was totally unexpected. I would even say it shocked me.

"I started with an old Harley," I explained. "I rebuilt it as a teenager, and moved up from there. I've got the two customized choppers, a partly redone Indian Chief Classic, and that one you're beside is an Ultralow."

Cass went to the smaller bike automatically. I watched her run her fingers along the smooth leather seat, and along the white body. I was both pleased by, and envious of, her obvious admiration.

The motorcycles—and the Parisienne—were my only truly personal indulgences. Everything else went into the business. The delight on Cass's face made me wish I had spent even more.

"Who rides these?" she wanted to know.

"I do."

"Alone?"

I shrugged. I had never found anyone who wanted to share the experience with me. And I had never found anyone worth sharing it with, either.

Impulsively, I reached up to the enormous key ring on the wall. I pulled down a big key and walked over to Cass.

"Here," I said.

She frowned, and I reached out to smooth the little wrinkles her expression made on her forehead.

"Put out your hand," I commanded, and when she obeyed, I pressed the key into her palm. "When this is done, I will teach you how to ride. But for now, let's go get paid, okay?"

She nodded and inhaled deeply. I steeled myself for our debut as I led her back to Leo's warehouse "office."

The building was nearly dark on the inside, and it smelled heavily of cigar smoke, as it usually did. I could hear men laughing and talking from somewhere else in the building. I guided Cass through a narrow corridor and into an open room. I watched her as she tried not to look interested in her surroundings. Her face went still as she tried even harder not to notice as all eyes turned to us. Lazy ceiling fans twirled above us, and the table full of men with cards in their hands were almost silent.

Three women, scantily clad and heavily made up, were serving drinks and giggling. They were working girls—I didn't doubt it for a second. I gave them a disgusted look and stepped a little closer to Cass.

"Is this what you guys do with my money when I'm not around?" I asked.

No one responded.

Cass plastered a half-smile on her face, and stood on her tiptoes so she could almost reach my ear. Her mouth tickled my skin, and my body responded automatically. I stifled a groan.

"This place stinks," she told me in a whisper. "Now laugh."

I chuckled quietly, and even I couldn't tell if it was fake or not.

"We weren't expecting you," said Leo, the man who ran their operation.

"Weren't you?" I countered coolly. "Then someone must not be doing his job."

There was a general grumble at my implication, and Cass gripped my hand a little tighter.

"It's not you, baby," I murmured into her hair. "They just don't like to be teased."

Leo appraised Cass slowly, and I my own grip tightened. He was generally cucumber cool, and his eyes only betrayed the slightest hint of curiosity as he assessed her. I casually slipped my hand out of Cass's and slid my arm around her waist.

"This looks boring, John," Cass complained. "Let's go back to your place again. I can think of something *way* better to do. Unless you think we've done it enough times already."

I wasn't expecting those words—or anything close to them—to come out of her mouth, and I covered my surprise with a big laugh. A couple of the other men actually laughed, too.

"I'm just surprised to see you here with a piece of merchandise on your arm," Leo stated.

My pent-up anger got the better of me. Billy's comments, Monato's attitude, Vance's information—it bubbled up, and there wasn't anything I could do stop myself.

I twisted away from Cass quickly, shot across the room and put my hand around Leo's throat. I saw at least four of the six men in the room draw weapons. One of the overdone women squealed, and another dropped her drink. I ignored them all.

"She is *not* a piece of merchandise," I said through clenched teeth.

"What is she?" Leo asked as he eyed Cass, seeming not to care that I was about to choke the life out of him.

"An opportunity," Cass replied artfully. "Or an opportunist, depending on how you look at things."

A few more of the men laughed, and one of the tables resumed their card game. With a boldness I was sure Cass didn't really feel, she sauntered over to me and placed her hand on my arm. I was betting she could feel the tension there, even through my jacket.

"Aren't you going to introduce me to your friends?" she asked.

I released Leo's neck and pulled her close. I had to find a release, so I leaned down and kissed her—hard. She closed her eyes right before I closed mine, and she sank into my embrace. I wished immediately that we didn't have audience. Putting on a show or not, my blood was heating up. Desire licked through my body as I gripped her soft hair in one of my fists. When I finally let her go, there was a round of applause in the room, and Cass buried her face in my chest.

"Very good," I murmured into her hair.

Did she know my momentary passion was anything but feigned?

"Gentlemen, this is Cass. The new love of my life," I announced.

"You gonna marry this one?" Leo asked.

"This one," Cass scoffed. "How many of us have there been?"

"None like you, Cass," I replied sincerely, and I saw one of the men roll his eyes.

Cass lifted her hand, showing off her ring, and spoke conspiratorially to the whole room. "The only problem with husbands is the second that ring is on your finger, they just start thinking of you as piece of property. And *I'm* not that kind of girl."

No one said a word, and I waited to see if she'd gone a little too far. One of the working girls pouted, and another shot Cass the evil eye. But even without that, there was an odd vibe in the room. I couldn't quite put my finger on where it was coming from.

"Cass," I said finally. "I'd like to you to meet my team of professionals and some of my business associates. This is Gary, my money man, and—"

She cut me off. "Dopey, Happy, and Sneezy. Don't tell me their names. Just tell me about their bank accounts."

"Thinking about trading him in already?" Leo joked.

"Are you kidding?" Cass responded with a grin. "Have you seen the size of his…"

My jaw just about dropped as she clapped her hands over her mouth and giggled.

"I'm not good with names," she confessed. "The only reason I remember *his* is that it's almost the same as my sister's—Jeannette."

She pointed at me and winked.

Leo grinned. "And is your sister as charming as you are?"

"She might've been at one point," Cass answered. "But she's been dead a long time. Let me know if you figure out a way to get in touch with her. She still owes me some money. And a boyfriend."

My arms—which were still around her—relaxed ever so slightly. I was still pretty wound up, but things were going way better than I could've possibly planned.

Chapter Seventeen

After pouting a little about not being allowed to sit in John's lap, I settled into the chair he gave me, and pretended to play on his phone. He'd made a show of letting me know that the data was *off*, and I took that to mean there were rules in place about communicating with the outside world during the business meeting.

I wasn't as interested in the business itself as I was in the men's reaction to me. I was rather pleased with myself, and aside from John's sudden kiss—which left me breathless for real—and the awkward mention of my sister—I cursed myself for that—I was certain that I played my part to a tee.

Seeing the three girls there, dressed in ass-baring skirts and spiked heels, intimidated me for just a minute. And I felt inspired to channel my inner goddess.

I'd recalled the time I'd sneaked into Jeannette's room and tried on one of her club outfits. The dress was short, with a scooped neckline. It hugged my curves, showed off my legs, and made me feel years older. When I looked in the mirror, I went from feeling like the usual beige I was to the vibrant, multihued version of myself I could become.

She caught me, of course. She came into the room as I twirled my fifteen-year-old self around, basking in the idea that I looked so good.

"Hey!" Jeannette hollered. "Take it off."

I turned to her guiltily. Her eyes were bloodshot, and she was stumbling even though it was the middle of the day.

"Why?" I replied defiantly. "If it's good enough for you, it's good enough for me."

My sister threw her hands up. "Nothing about my life is good enough for you."

Something in her voice—the combination of defeat and desperation—made me soften. I peeled the dress off and slipped my jeans back on.

"I'm sorry," I said softly.

But Jeannette was already passed out on the bed. I was going to toss the dress down beside her, but as it slipped through my fingers, its alluring sparkle drew me back in. At the last second, I grabbed it and hid it in my closet. And when things started to get really bad with Jeannette, I would pull it out and look at it, knowing somewhere underneath my Plain Jane exterior was that bold, sexy girl.

I took that remembered feeling, held onto it tightly, and transferred it into my interactions with John's associates.

If I hadn't been so terrified, I might've actually kind of enjoyed it.

I was also curious about the dynamic between these men and John. His business associates, he'd called them. If I had to guess, I would say that while John was somehow in charge, most of the guys in the room didn't answer directly to him. With the exception of Leo, they were too standoffish for me to think they worked closely with him. Maybe the card game was a pretence for something else, too, although I didn't know what. Then again, maybe it just gave them something to do.

I started up another game of Mahjong on John's phone, and only half-listened to what was going on in the room.

"What're the numbers looking like?" John was asking. "You have my payments?"

"Things look about the same. I've got most of it, even though you're two days early," Leo replied. "You want details?"

John nodded and gestured at the money man. "Get them, Gary."

He was young, and dressed in a business suit. He pulled out a briefcase and glanced nervously at me, then around at the men in the room.

"Are you sure you want to do this with her here?" he asked.

There was a flurry of movement, and then John punched Gary square in the face with no warning. I held in a gasp. Even though I had been watching him overreact for over a day, the sudden and violent act caught me by surprise. None of the men even blinked as Gary covered his now bleeding nose. Leo pulled a napkin out from somewhere and handed it to the younger man.

"I think you fucking broke it!" Gary howled.

"Serves you right," Leo muttered.

"Have I *ever* given you permission to question me?" John demanded.

"No," Gary whimpered.

"Have I ever even given you a *reason* to?"

"No."

"Do you like your job, Gary? Do I pay you well?

Would you make this kind of money at some downtown accounting firm?" John asked.

"No, I—"

John cut him off. "I've been going easy on you because you're new to the business. But I think I've been going a little too easy. Maybe on everyone."

I tapped furiously on the phone's screen, and avoided looking up.

"Gary—and anyone else who has a concern—has a choice," John announced. "He can treat Cass as an extension of *me*. He can say anything in front of her he would say in front of me unless I say otherwise. I will personally vouch for her. Anyone who doesn't like it, can leave. Now."

Leo was the only one who glanced my way. His eyes were on me, and he was likely wondering if his boss had been blinded by his interest in me.

All of the others just shuffled uncomfortably and avoided looking at Gary.

But no one left.

"Somebody clean up all this goddamned blood while Gary gets the numbers out," John commanded. "And somebody else tell me what the Hell these girls are doing in here in the middle of a business meeting?"

"You brought your own girl in," a familiar voice pointed out.

I looked up. It only took me a second to place the man. He was Ramirez, the discredited doctor who had put in the IV port while I'd been passed out in John's car. I hadn't noticed him at the card table before, and I assumed he had come in after.

"Doc." If John was surprised to see him, he gave nothing away.

"He says he's *marrying* this one," Leo said.

"When?"

"I'd do it now, if I could," John replied.

My heart jumped in my chest, but I refused to look up.

"We can do that," Leo stated.

John laughed. "Are you an ordained minister now, Leo? Casinos *and* churches?"

I stopped fiddling around on the phone, and was listening intently. All of the eyes in the room focused on me.

"Nobody needs a church to get married anymore," Leo said easily. "In fact…I keep the paperwork in my filing cabinet for impromptu occasions like this."

"You do not," I said with what I hoped would pass for a spontaneous giggle.

"Oh, but I do," Leo told me seriously.

There was the briefest of pauses and then John was pulling me to my feet.

"All right, Leo. Say the words while Gary gets the papers," he commanded.

He met my terrified gaze with a wink. My head swam, and from somewhere in the thickness of my mind, Leo laughed and called out some words that vaguely resembled wedding vows. Then there was silence.

"Well? Do you?" John asked me.

The men laughed, and John nudged me.

"Are you kidding?" I heard myself say. "Pass up on the opportunity to land this guy? With all of you as my witnesses? The mere possibility of alimony alone is worth it."

"So you do?" Leo wanted to know.

"I do," I replied.

John planted a quick kiss on my lips and shoved a piece of paper at me. I signed it woodenly and plopped myself back in my chair.

"All right," John said. "Now that all that's settled, let's get back to work so I can take my wife on a proper honeymoon. And ask the girls to go. They don't need to know the intricate details of my business."

"These are Monato's girls," Leo told him. "And he's not a guy I want to insult."

I felt my heart stop.

These are Monato's girls?

I glanced up at them and then back down at my hands.

"They were a gift," Leo said not-quite calmly.

"Is that right?" John replied angrily.

"Monato was *here,* John," Leo told him. "We're a little worried."

I braced myself for another punching session, but John just looked at him. Then he stood up and paced the room for a minute before making a sweeping gesture and shouting, "Go! If any of you want to get paid, get *out!* All of you except Leo."

Everyone scrambled out, and John turned to me. His eyes flashed with a mix of anger and worry.

"Did I tell *you* to stay?"

"You didn't tell me to go," I countered.

He stalked over to me with his hand raised and I lifted my chin defiantly.

Try it, my expression said, but inwardly I was cowering. It was the first time John had directed his supposedly fake anger toward me, and now that I had seen some of what he was capable of, I was scared.

I gasped as he came toward me with his palm open. Even if there had been a way for me to get away fast enough, I couldn't have moved. I was frozen in my seat. He reached back and swung with full force. Then he stopped, just an inch from my face. I waited, motionless, with my heart pounding so hard I thought he could probably see it through my shirt. He leaned down and his eyes were apologetic as he kissed me gently on the mouth. He lingered there for a moment. His lips were soft, and tempting, and I automatically reached my arms up and wrapped them around his neck. He made a small noise in his throat as I pulled him closer.

Leo coughed, and John let me go.

"And *that* is why I need you to wait in the other room," John said loudly.

I was too out of breath to argue.

Chapter Eighteen

I didn't want her to go. Not really. I realized I was worried about letting her out of my sight for even a second, and I had to force myself to not stare after her. Something close to anxiety gripped me, I shoved it away.

"What was Monato doing here?" I demanded.

Leo shrugged. Sometimes the man's casual indifference grated on me.

"He came in, cool as ice, and offered us a deal," Leo told me.

"What was the deal?"

"All our debt to you. Plus a million even. For a girl with blonde hair and a bad attitude," he explained.

I fought for control.

"A million," I stated. "Split how many ways?"

"My guys. Two of my hired men. So ten altogether," Leo said. "If you don't count Gary. And I don't, since you pay him directly."

I examined the other man carefully. He was an unusual kind of businessman. His casinos did well on their own, and the two I had backed always saw return. Leo was never in a hurry, never got rattled, and never made overly quick decisions.

Most of us have an admittedly short fuse.

"So one hundred thousand each," I said.

"And a vacation from paying you," Leo added. "He

said he'd pay you your usual fees directly."

"A vacation," I repeated. "So what did you tell him?"

"To get the fuck out."

I let myself smile just a little bit. I would've loved to have seen Monato's reaction. I was sure Leo would've told him in his typically calm way.

"Some of the men were interested," Leo said. "In the girls as well as the money. He left them as a show of good faith."

It explained the tense vibe in the room. My anxiety spiked again as I pictured Cass alone with some of the "interested" men.

"Which ones wanted to take the deal?" I wanted to know.

"I can't tell you that."

"No, I suppose not," I sighed.

"They won't move right now," Leo told me. "Not while you're here. But after you've gone it's hard to say what they'll consider doing. There's more than a few loose cannons on my team. And when I start collecting fees again for next month's payments…"

"Do you have that little control?" I asked irritably.

"You and I both know I'm not the kind of boss who follows his guys around monitoring their behaviour. Especially when money is involved. Sometimes it's better not to know," he replied easily.

I grunted. He was right, even if I didn't like it.

"Thanks for keeping me informed, Leo," I said.

"Mind if I ask what's up with you and Monato?" Leo asked.

"I don't like him," I replied.

"I know the guy's an idiot—we all do—but with

you, it seems personal," Leo stated.

I pushed down my instant anger. I'd already put my hands on the guy once. He'd taken it in stride, but I didn't want to push my luck twice in one day. I forced myself to shrug.

"You heard what he did to Cass," I offered. "Or at least I'm assuming he gave you his part of the story."

"He just said you were encroaching on his territory. That you'd jumped in when he was clearly interested."

"The man came into *my* club. Was he really expecting to leave with one of my guests over his shoulder and not have to face the consequences?"

"I also heard that you just met the girl yourself," Leo replied.

"Love at first sight," I said.

Leo tapped his chin thoughtfully. "I'm in the card business. You're in the finance business. Monato is in the girl business. I don't always agree with his methods, but interfering can be…"

"*Bad* for business?" I filled in.

"Pick another girl," he suggested with a nod, and held up the signed marriage license.

"I can't."

It was the truth, and I was certain Leo could tell I meant it. We'd had enough dealings together to know each other at least that well. He lifted his hand in a surrendering gesture. I yanked Gary's briefcase open and tossed the accounting requisitions to Leo.

I wanted nothing more than to get paid and get Cass out of there are quickly as I could.

Chapter Nineteen

I had shuffled out of the big room through the door where I'd seen the other men and women go, and then I'd paused just outside, sagging against the wall.

In all of my time with Dean, both as a married couple and even before, I had never felt like that. When John kissed me, my whole body heated up in response. I forgot that anyone was watching. I even forgot we were just pretending.

I touched my lips with my fingers. Why did he continued to affect me so deeply? Pretending be his girl—*wife,* I corrected—wasn't easy. But it wasn't hard, either. At least not so far. There was something about the man that made me lose control. And worse, he made me *want* to lose it. I was giving in to that urge. I had signed the papers without even making sure they could be discarded. I was pushing aside self-restraint and common sense, and acting on instinct instead.

Maybe that's the problem.

I was too used to keeping myself contained, and my impulsive behaviour was letting more than a little excitement bubble over my self-imposed wall. It left me vulnerable. It made me respond to John in a way I hadn't expected. It made me slip up and talk about Jeanette to a roomful of strangers.

I shook my head to clear away the lingering effects of John's kiss. In spite of his apologetic look as he forced me to leave, I was apprehensive.

What kind of men were these, that he would need to be so violent with them? Did they really need that kind of control in order to behave? Or was that just the kind of man John really was? And now…what were they going to be like when I was alone with them? It was one thing to maintain the charade with him there to act as a buffer. It was a whole other to carry it on my own.

I convinced myself to stop leaning on the wall, and walked down the hall, following sounds of men talking. I listened to them through the door. Their voices were deep. Raucous. Intimidating. One of the hired ladies giggled, and all of the men laughed loudly, too. It did nothing to ease my tension.

C'mon, I cajoled myself. *You can do this.*

I took a deep, measured breath, and made my entrance.

"Hello, ladies and gentlemen," I greeted with a grin. "It seems I've been demoted."

One of the women—the one who had sneered at me at the poker table—walked over to me and grabbed my hand. I almost recoiled from her as she ran her manicured hand over mine.

"Pretty rock," she said.

I met her gaze as coolly as I could manage. She was my age, or maybe even younger. Her eyes were red-rimmed, and I guessed instantly that she was high. Her clothes barely covered her assets, but they weren't cheap. She caught my scrutiny and shrugged.

"Baby," one of the men called, and she finally let my hand go to attend to whatever it was he needed.

I glanced around the room. My eyes settled on the

money man. He gave me a dark look from behind his bloody nose. He put down his ice pack and sneered.

"I knew it wouldn't last," he said.

I did my best to look impassive.

"Still. I'd rather be in my shoes than yours," I remarked.

"And I'm sure getting in your *shoes* is the furthest thing from John's mind at the moment," Gary countered.

I leaned closer to him. "Trust me. *I* have nothing to worry about."

"I feel like you're threatening me," Gary said. "And I'm not sure why you think that's okay. Grown men are more afraid of John—hell, even of me—than you are. Care to explain that at all?"

I thought fast. I hadn't really been expecting to have to defend my obnoxious comments. I remembered that John had implied that the men should have been expecting his presence—even though he had arrived ahead of schedule.

"John doesn't trust you," I whispered. "He thinks *someone* knows a bit too much. He knows it's not me. He knows it's not Leo…"

Gary's eyes widened, and I realized my bullshit ploy was probably close to the truth.

"Right," he said sarcastically. "From what I hear, he's the one who's practically stalking the whole crew, following our every move. Following Monato around, too. And even that guy thought it showed a lack of faith."

My skin crawled at the name.

"John trusts me. Explicitly," I added. "What about *you,* Gary? You talk to Monato a lot?"

"You're not a regular player," he said, deflecting my obvious implication. "What are you in this for? Your clothes are rich. You're obviously attached to the boss. But something doesn't sit right."

"That might just be what you had for lunch, Gary," interrupted a calm voice.

I glanced up at the man who had joined us. It was Ramirez again. Did he know I recognized him?

Gary looked at him uncertainly.

"*You* believe her story?" he asked.

"What's to believe?" the Doc replied dismissively. "You can tell just from looking at them where this is going."

He sounded so sincere that I just about let my careful mask slip. I was glad the two men were looking at each other instead of at me.

"The man's always been an unfeeling bastard as best I could tell. He's got revenge on the brain," Gary stated.

The Doc raised his eyebrows. "Revenge? For what? On who?"

Gary shrugged. "Dunno. But I heard one of the other guys say it, and I don't doubt it. Nobody can be that driven, but have zero feelings."

"Maybe," Ramirez replied in a considering voice. "But as far as Cass is concerned…he certainly doesn't seem unfeeling anymore."

Gary rolled his eyes and turned back to me. "All I know is Monato was clearly after you. Is still after you. Who knows why. But John saw it, and had to get in on the action. Marrying you at a card table? We'll just see if that sticks."

I opened my mouth to say something—I don't

know what—but out of nowhere someone cracked me on the head, and I fell forward, face first into Gary's lap. Someone tossed a bag over my head, and I had to gasp for breath until someone rolled me over. I landed on the ground with a heavy thump.

Shouts of surprise and anger filled the room. Three resounding pops carried through the air, and I was immediately sure they were gunshots.

"The girls," someone growled. "*That* girl."

Monato.

It was him. I knew it.

Rough hands grabbed my ankles and dragged me across the floor. I tried to kick, and earned a not-gentle kick in the kidneys.

"In here," Monato said.

Whoever was pulling me along let me go without ceremony. Someone secured my hands and yanked off the hood. I blinked rapidly as my eyes adjusted to the relative darkness. I was in a small room full of racks of fabric. And I was face to face with the greasy little would-be kidnapper. He smiled. I looked away, and he grabbed my chin forcing me to meet his gaze. He was wearing thick gloves, and the feel of them made me cringe.

"I don't think so," he told me. "I want you to watch this so you know what's coming."

The three hookers came stumbling into the room, followed closely by a gun-wielding man in a ski mask.

"Strip," Monato told them.

I tried to look away, and he cuffed my cheek with the back of his hand. Tears started, and with my hands tied, I couldn't even wipe them away. The three young women undressed down to their underwear, quickly and wordlessly, and stood facing Monato.

"String them up," he said to the man in the ski mask, before he turned back to me. "I *like* these girls. They work for me, and they don't complain."

I watched helplessly as they allowed themselves to be bound. Monato pulled knife from his pocket and dragged it along one of the girl's throats. She blinked, but didn't move.

"Please stop," I whispered.

"No."

Monato went to the girls and slowly, almost lovingly wrapped a long piece of red cord around each of their necks. Then he marched them over to one of the racks of cloth and began winding the cord around the highest metal shelf.

"Please," I said.

"No."

The girls finally seemed to finally clue in that something unpleasant was going to happen, to realize that this wasn't just some game. One of them tried to kick Monato in the shins, but he sidestepped her easily. Another started to scream, but he tightened the cord so she couldn't do anything but choke. The third attempted to flee, and Monato laughed as the rack shuddered and forced her to stop abruptly.

Then the cruel little man slid over to pull on the thick wire, securing it so the girls were suspended and had to stand on their tiptoes to keep breathing. He turned back to me.

"They'll get tired soon enough.

I heard myself whimper in response.

"Take your clothes off," he said.

I shook my head because I didn't trust my voice.

Monato tugged the cords again, and the three women gagged.

"Now."

With shaking hands, I struggled to pull off my shirt and then my pants. My body didn't want to cooperate. When I finally did manage to drop my clothes to the floor, I shivered uncontrollably.

Monato appraised me slowly.

"What a waste," he said, and shrugged. "I just wish it didn't have to be quick like this."

And he was beside me, wrapping the red cord around my neck tightly. He used it to yank me roughly across the room, then he took the free end of the wire and tossed it over a metal beam above our heads. I felt myself lift up, and I kicked, trying desperately to maintain my footing. I failed.

Breathe.

I tried to obey the command that came from my brain, but after just a few moments, the world slid away.

Chapter Twenty

I knew something was off as soon as Billy came running through the door. He looked pissed off, and he was out of breath. I stood up automatically.

"Cass," he wheezed.

I glanced at Leo and replied as calmly as I could manage. "What about her?"

Billy put his hand on his chest and inhaled deeply. "Where is she?"

"What?"

"Where the fuck is your *wife*?"

"I sent her out so I could talk to Leo."

Billy glanced at the other man. "I'd like to talk to him, too. His guards should be shot. If they haven't been already."

Leo raised both of his eyebrows.

"They kept *me* out," Billy elaborated. "But let Monato in."

My heart dropped, and I had a moment of utter panic. I rounded on Leo. Forget shooting the guards, I wanted to kill *him*. But I turned back to Billy. I needed find Cass more, to make sure she was safe.

"Go," I commanded, and drew my gun.

Leo put his hands up wordlessly, and I followed him out into the hall and down the corridor. We stopped in front of a closed door, and Billy moved in front of us. He leaned against it, listening intently.

"Nothing," he said under his breath.

He swung the door open and called out, "Coming in. Back the hell up or get shot!"

He moved cautiously into the room, and I pushed Leo forward with my gun at his back.

Four men were lying unconscious on the floor under a table. They'd been roped together with thick wire.

"Where the hell is she?" I hollered. "Where's Cass?"

"She's not in here," Billy told me. "At least not that I can see."

"Jesus!" I swore

I kicked over a chair and rounded on Leo again.

"I thought you had control over the situation," I said coldly.

"I thought I did, too," Leo replied, sounding unconcerned.

He moved toward the men under the table and untied some of the knots. I grabbed him by the sleeve.

"What are you doing?" I demanded.

The other man shrugged. "I'm going to wake them up. See what they know."

"Don't bother," I said. "If I find out one of them let something happen to my wife, I won't be responsible for my actions."

"Hey, John?" Billy was frowning.

"What?"

"Where are the girls?"

"Maybe Monato took them back," Leo offered.

A sudden thump from the other side of the room caught my attention. I lifted my gun.

"What's back there, Leo?" I asked.

"Storage closet," he told me with a casual shrug. "Linens."

I shoved him out of my way and stalked over to the wide door at the end of the room. I twisted the handle carefully, keeping my weapon ready. I swung the door open slowly, and stared into a mass of silk cloth, hanging from a series of racks and wide metal bars. I pushed the fabric aside and bile rose in my throat.

All three of the women who had been brought in for entertainment purposes were hanging from one of the racks. They were stripped down to their underwear, eyes closed. Each of them had a zip cord fastened tightly around her neck. I couldn't tell if they were alive or dead.

There was a blood-spattered knife at their feet, and without thinking, I grabbed it and cut the girls down. They landed, unmoving, on the floor.

"They alive?" Billy asked.

"Maybe," I replied doubtfully.

Goddammit. Where is Cass? I clenched my teeth desperately.

A bang came from the far end of the closet and I turned my attention toward it. I pushed aside more reams of the silk, and drew in a sharp breath.

Oh, God, no.

I froze. Cass was there, eyes closed, feet dangling. Her pants and tank top were in a pile beneath her. A piece of paper was pinned to her bra.

MINE, it read in bold capital letters.

She moved weakly. One of her legs came up, thumped against a box there, and slid down again.

Billy moved before I could even react. He grabbed her around the waist, pulled a knife from his pocket, and sliced through the zip cord.

"Gimme your shirt, John," he ordered as he lowered her to the floor.

I just stared at him.

"Now!" he yelled.

I finally shook myself, yanked off the shirt, and handed it over. Billy pulled it onto Cass, and pressed his ear against her chest.

"Breathing," he said tersely.

She groaned almost inaudibly, and I felt crazed mix of emotions. Guilt. Anger. Relief. I stared down at Cass's beautiful face and growled.

I stormed out. Leo was sitting beside his men, working on their ropes.

"I told you to stop that."

"I don't think finding their inside man is going to be a problem," Leo told me, and handed me a Polaroid.

"Shit," I said.

It was a picture of Gary, my very own money man, with a knife—the same one I had used to release the girls, in fact—sticking out of his abdomen. A telltale sign was hanging around his neck, too.

MINE.

Bile rise in my throat. Even though he had betrayed me, I was responsible. I'd taken Gary in after one of the bosses had tossed him out. He wasn't much more than a kid.

I went back to Billy and tossed the picture at him.

"We are going to find Monato. And we are going to kill him," I told him. "Wait here."

I spun on my heel and strode past Leo again, ignoring the curious look on his face, then marched out into the hall. I kept going until I came to an emergency exit. I shoved the door open and took a deep breath of fresh air before reaching into my pocket and drawing out the slim, pink phone.

I had been going to give it back to Cass, to show her I trusted her. But right now I needed it for another reason.

I hit speed dial one and waited.

"Oh my God!" Blair answered. "When you said you'd call me in a few days, I didn't think you meant literally. I was getting ready to call the police!"

"Please don't do that," I replied.

"Um, *hello*?"

I smiled a little in spite of my terrifically bad mood.

"This is John."

"No shit. This is Blair."

"Yeah, I called you," I reminded her.

"With Cass's phone," she pointed out loudly. "If you've killed her and are using one of her boobs as a purse, so help me, I will hunt you down myself."

I burst out laughing and it probably sounded a little hysterical. I fought to control it.

"It won't be so funny when I make my own purse out of your—"

I cut her off before she could put an image in my head I'd never get rid of.

"I need your help," I told her.

"Carnations, not roses. Peppermints, not chocolates. That's all I'm telling you," Blair replied firmly.

I cleared my throat. "I'm not much of a romantic guy. But I was hoping for something a little more dramatic. I'd like to take Cass somewhere special."

Safe, I added mentally.

"Like…Vegas special?" she replied suspiciously.

"More special than that," I replied in a deadly serious voice. "I want to take her somewhere she would never expect, but somewhere she'd love."

Blair went surprisingly silent. She was probably trying to process what kind of man I was, and how much of a break I deserved.

"You still there?" I asked after a full minute of silence.

"I'm here," she said reluctantly.

"Do you think you can suggest something?"

"I swear to God if you even *think* about hurting her, I will cut you," Blair threatened.

I chuckled. "I'm the guy who saved her, remember?"

"I'll be the judge of that. I'll need to give you the keys to the cabin. And a map. It's not on GPS yet. And we'll do it in person or not at all," she said. "Can you meet me in twenty minutes?"

"A cabin?" I managed to get out.

Perfect. Isolated, hard to get to, and unrelated to anything to do with my business.

I hastily committed the address of the coffee shop to memory, sent a text to Billy, and took off.

Chapter Twenty-One

My throat felt like it had been burned, sanded down, and stuck through with a thorny branch, all at once. I tried to clear it, and ended up doubled over in hacking pain.

"Hey there."

I blinked up at the sound of Billy's gruff voice.

"You're not dead," he said.

I opened my mouth to speak, and the feel of air rushing in made me gag. Billy handed me a bottled water and I drank from it slowly and carefully.

"I don't think I'm alive, either," I croaked.

"When you're ready to sit up, let me know," he replied, and I realized I was more or less lying in his lap.

I shifted my body so I could prop myself up. I leaned against the wall and closed my eyes.

"What happened?" I asked in a whisper.

"I hoped you were gonna tell me."

I frowned, trying to remember. I had been talking to Gary, and there had been a lot of shouting, and a man in a mask had burst through the door. The rest was a blur of red rope and flailing limbs and cruel eyes.

"Monato…I'm not sure…" I said, trailing off as I remembered the coldness in his eyes. "I think he was trying to kill me."

Billy grunted irritably. I turned my head and

immediately wished that I hadn't. The three hookers were slumped together in the middle of the storage room.

"Oh, God."

I leaned over and dry heaved.

"Are they dead?" I asked.

"Leo!" Billy hollered without answering me. "Get these fucking girls out of here."

"Can't!"

"Why the hell not?"

The heavyset man popped his head into the closet and gave us a helpless shrug.

"Police are on their way," he told us.

"What? What the hell for?" Billy demanded.

Leo shrugged again. "Someone called them. Maybe your friend Monato is trying to stir the pot. Got the news on my scanner."

"Does he *want* to get caught?" Billy sounded utterly confused.

"Monato was wearing gloves," I croaked as I remembered the feeling I'd had when he touched me with them.

"Shit," Billy said. "John's prints are all over this room now. On the girls…"

"Put on your pants, Cass. We gotta get outta here. Fast."

I looked down at my legs stupidly, realizing they were bare. I tried to move them, but they felt like rubber. Billy grabbed my arm and yanked me forcefully to my feet. I stumbled a little, and caught myself on the wall.

"Leo, bring my goddamned car to the closest door," Billy commanded.

I tried unsuccessfully to slide my feet into the black pants I'd been wearing. The older man made an annoyed sound in the back of his throat and ripped the pants out of my hands.

"Forget it," he said, and scooped up my shirt and shoes, too. "Let's go."

I clung to his arm, and walked behind him to the now-familiar sedan. He did up my seatbelt for me and drove the car through the parking lot, keeping his eyes on the road. We went out a different way than we came in, avoided the main entrance, and continued along a gravel road that ran below the highway. After a few minutes, Billy eased the car behind a natural embankment and waited. He said nothing as four police cars sped past us on the main road. I watched nervously as the flashing lights went by.

What would happen to John if he got stuck in the middle of this? And where had he gone? I worried.

"They can't see us from up there," Billy muttered as he put the car back into drive.

"Okay."

He pulled onto the road and turned on the radio. I watched out the window while holding my raw throat.

Where in God's name was he taking me now?

Chapter Twenty-Two

Even if I hadn't seen her once before, I would've been able to identify Cass's friend from a mile away. She looked just like she sounded on the phone—brassy hair, skin tight jeans, and perpetually snapping gum. She was also tapping a ring full of keys on her knee, and looking around suspiciously.

I approached her slowly, plastering my best nice-guy smile on my face. It required some effort. The drive out to the coffee shop hadn't calmed me down at all. It had only served to make me more tense. This woman probably knew Cass better than anyone. If she had any idea of what I had just put her best friend through…I forcefully shoved the thought aside. I wouldn't give her a reason to become suspicious. I had to concentrate on getting this woman to trust me enough to cooperate with me so I could make Cass safe.

"Blair?" I said softly, and slid into the seat facing her.

"Well…poop on toast," she replied. "You are *not* what I expected."

I watched her take in my exposed, tattooed forearms, and squint at my dark sunglasses.

I let myself chuckle. "Thank you."

I pushed the sunglasses onto my head, and tried to look as innocent and as non-intimidating as I could manage. It's no mean feat at my size. I could tell she was trying hard to read me. She continued to bounce the keys and scrutinize my face. I stifled a sigh. What was she looking for? The hero on the white horse? A clue as to why her best friend had run off with me on some seeming whim?

She's going to be sorely disappointed.

The jangling of the keys intensified, and I placed my hand over top of hers to silence it. Blair pulled herself away quickly. She clutched the key ring to her chest and narrowed her eyes at me. I didn't have time for games. I needed to get Cass somewhere before Monato realized she wasn't dead. I wanted to rip the keys away from her and be done with it.

I went for charming instead.

I let my eyes soften and raised an eyebrow. I gave her my best crooked smile.

"I'm kinda in a hurry to impress Cass," I told her.

"She's never in a hurry."

I gritted my teeth and held my smile in place. "Do you believe in love at first sight?"

"No."

"I just really want to surprise her," I said mildly. "And maybe sweep her off her feet."

"You wanna give me a better explanation?" Blair asked without changing her expression.

I sighed. Charming wasn't working. And maybe Blair didn't want to bother with games either.

"No," I replied with a shrug. "I don't have time for an explanation. Nor do I particularly want to give you one."

"Finally," Blair said, visibly relaxing. "Some honesty. Is this about the other guy at the club? The one who she said drugged her?"

"Yes. And I promise you, I only have Cass's best interests at heart," I told her truthfully. "I might not even be the best option for that. But I'm the only one she has at the moment."

I put my hand out, and Blair dropped the keys into it. I leaned over the table and placed a quick kiss on her cheek.

"Thank you," I said sincerely, and left her staring after me.

I was no less angry with myself, but I was happy to be on the move.

As soon as I got out to the car, though, I realized I had a problem. The big, red Parisienne was possibly the least inconspicuous car on the planet. I was going to have to find something more appropriate, and I wasn't going to be able to use any of my usual connections.

"Nice car."

I turned and saw Blair had followed me to the parking lot.

"Stands out, doesn't it?" I replied wryly.

She nodded. "And it's probably not going to be great on the road up to the cabin, either."

"What do you drive?"

"A truck."

I eyed her speculatively, and she shook her head.

"Uh uh. No way," she stated.

"Please?"

"I said no way. I'm not driving that *thing* around," Blair told me firmly as she gestured to my car.

I felt myself deflate. The events of the last forty-eight hours were catching up to me in a big way.

"Stop making that sad face," Blair said.

"Sorry."

She sighed. "All right. I might know somebody who's looking to unload something that's a little less…obvious. How much cash can you get ahold of?"

I pretended to shrug casually. "Some."

She pulled out her phone, and in less than thirty minutes, my Parisienne was parked in her mechanic's garage and I was on the road in my new vehicle.

Chapter Twenty-Three

Billy was standing outside of his car, smoking and glancing at his watch. I watched him light one cigarette off the other, then tense up as the sound of an engine cut through the otherwise still air. So far three cars had come and gone, driving past the nearly invisible turnoff without slowing.

This one was different.

The rumble of tires on gravel got closer, and a black Jeep came cruising around the corner at well above the speed limit. It spun to a stop right in front of us, and John hopped out.

He went straight to Billy, and spoke to him in a low voice. I couldn't hear them, but it looked like they were arguing. Billy tossed his cigarette down and ground it out aggressively before stalking to the car and yanking my door open.

"Out," he said in an audibly angry voice. "Get in the Jeep."

I obeyed without speaking. The intensity of the situation and the violence I'd experienced, earlier coupled with the horrific outcome, was starting to wear on me.

I climbed into the raised up vehicle, and did up my seatbelt. I saw my suitcase was in the back seat.

John said a few final words to Billy, and strapped himself into the driver's seat without looking at me. He put the Jeep in gear and peeled away without looking back.

His face was dark as he drove, and even in the muted twilight, I could see that all the lines of his body were tense with anger.

"Do you want to talk?" I asked hesitantly.

He was staring out the windshield with his eyes narrowed, and the sound of my voice made him jump. I watched him try to control his expression.

"Talk about what?" he replied in a strained voice.

"Anything," I offered.

"Where do you want to start? With what was done to…" he swallowed thickly. "The girls at the warehouse? With you being tied up and locked up right under my nose?"

His tone made me cringe.

He made a sudden turn, and I was thankful for my seatbelt as we hit a patch of loose gravel and the tires spun. John pretended not to notice the momentary loss of control. He held the steering wheel straight and maneuvered the Jeep up the increasingly dark road.

"You want to know why I saved you from Monato?" he asked in a harsh voice.

He took another quick turn, and I yelped a bit as I cracked my head on the side window. John braked, then lurched to a stop.

"Cass, I'm sorry," he said.

He sounded as regretful as he did furious.

"I'm all right," I replied.

He put his head down on the steering wheel, and I saw the anger leave his body.

"I seem to have forgotten how to have a normal...conversation," he told me.

For some reason, I had been expecting him to finish his sentence with the word *relationship* and my heart fluttered nervously.

"Cass, I was wrong," John said. "I can't be responsible for you. I shouldn't have assumed I could."

I reached out and put my hand on his arm. I was surprised a bit by his sudden and apparent vulnerability. He tensed again for a second as my skin met his, and then his shoulders fell again. My heart lurched in my chest, and I wished immediately that I was the one doing the protecting.

"For God's sake. This was supposed to be a *test*," he said. "And I practically got you killed. I thought I was keeping you safe, but I'm just making things worse. No one even knew I was coming to that meeting. I hadn't even told Leo."

"Someone is telling Monato where you'll be," I stated.

"What?"

"Gary, that money guy, he said something about you tracking Monato's every move," I told him. "What if he's tracking you, too?"

"You're probably right," he said, and it sounded more like *definitely* than probably.

For a second, he looked like he was going to say something else, but he just slammed his hand against the dashboard and pulled out his phone. He typed in a furious text, then turned back to me. His eyes were defeated.

"I don't seem to be doing anything right."

"What if you had just let Monato have me in the first place?" I asked gently. "Would that have been better?"

"I don't know."

"You don't know? Aren't you the one who told me he was in the business of trading women as a commodity?"

"He might not have tried to kill you if I hadn't got involved."

"There are things that are worse than being killed. And I'd rather be a part of a hundred of your failed tests than be involved with that man for one second," I told him.

"You sound so sure," he said, and there was a desperation in his voice that made my heart ache once again.

"Absolutely," I replied.

"All right," he said, sounding relieved, if not convinced.

He put the Jeep into drive again and when he pulled out a little more cautiously onto the road, I finally recognized the terrain.

"Where are you taking me?" I asked, even though I thought I might already know.

Chapter Twenty-Four

I pulled into the cabin's driveway and avoided Cass's eyes. I wanted to believe she wasn't angry at me. But it was hard. Especially when I was so pissed off at myself. She obviously knew where we were, but she didn't say a word as I carried her suitcase up to the cabin and dropped it on the front step.

She finally grabbed my hand and squeezed it.

"It'll be cold in there," Cass told me. "Do you mind grabbing some firewood from the shed? I'll get us set up inside."

"All right," I said, unable to disguise my relief.

I marched over to the shed. It was full of big logs, and empty of chopped wood, so I grabbed an axe and got to work.

As backwards as it seems, I've always found when I'm at the point of collapse, physical exertion can bring me back.

I swung the axe with all of my strength, and the wood splintered underneath my efforts.

I was suffering, and even I knew it.

I couldn't put into words how I was feeling. The sudden and overwhelming anguish I'd experienced when I believed Monato had taken Cass—it had almost undone me. I hadn't felt anything like it since Colin had died. And even so, those feelings were nothing compared to the guilt-riddled relief I'd experienced when I'd opened the storage closet and found her there, barely alive. If Leo hadn't been somewhere nearby, I might've collapsed right there.

I was impressed at how well Cass was holding up. I had subjected her to an awful lot over the past two days, and all she'd done to show it was to rub her eyes a little tiredly when I'd let her into the cabin. Even though she hadn't yet said a word about the fact that we were using her friend's parents' cabin as a hideout, she must be thinking about it. If anything, she'd seemed relieved to be in familiar surroundings.

I glanced up, and I could see her through one of the windows, sweeping and smiling.

She's doing better than I am, I admitted to myself as I took another wide chop at the unsuspecting wood.

The proof was in my near breakdown on the road.

What if she had died on my watch?

I pushed the disturbing thought aside and splintered some more kindling. But another one crept in.

A mole.

Cass had to be right. I hadn't considered it before because it hadn't mattered before. Because it was just me. With Cass in the picture… I inhaled and took another swing with the axe.

I looked up again, and saw that Cass had stepped onto the porch. She was shaking out blankets and pillows. I paused in my chopping to observe her performing the old fashioned domestic task. I relaxed as I watched her.

Monato thought she was dead, I reminded myself. *At least for now.*

So at least he had been placated temporarily. If he *had* been having me watched by someone other than

Gary, he'd have lost at least some of his motivation to do so. If I had a say in it at all, I would find Monato before he even realized Cass was alive.

Cass waved at me from behind a small cloud of dust.

"I think it's been a while since the place has been aired out!" she called. "You coming in soon?"

"In a minute," I told her with an only partly fake smile.

I finished taking out my aggression on the pile of logs, then loaded up my arms and went after her into the rustic house. It was my first real look inside. It was a traditional log house, decorated with kitschy charm. A huge, *clearly* fake fish, surrounded by old fashioned rods was mounted on one wall. A stuffed elk's head—maybe real, but probably not—looked out from above the single bedroom door. The curtains were made of red checkered cloth, and a cuckoo clock hung above the kitchen window. The whole thing made me grin.

"Don't worry," Cass said when she saw my face. "There's running water and even a toilet."

She had settled onto the futon and she was sitting with her legs curled up under a patchwork quilt. She had tucked back her long hair into a ponytail, too. Clad in my T-shirt and the flannel pants she'd found somewhere in the cabin, she looked perfectly at home.

I stuffed as much of the chopped wood into the fireplace as would fit, lit the kindling, and worked at getting it going.

"So…I take it you talked to Blair?" Cass asked.

"I saw her," I replied with a chuckle. "She's pretty protective of you."

"Yeah." Cass sounded a little sheepish, but her

smile got wider. "She's a good friend. Was she super mad?"

"Yes," I admitted as I tossed in some crumpled up newspaper and poked it around a bit. "More worried than anything. She called me a gorgeous hunk of a man, though."

"She did *not*!" Cass said.

I laughed. "Okay, maybe not. But for sure she was thinking it."

"More than likely."

When I was sure I had the flue open, and the fire stoked well enough, I joined her on the futon.

"Cass, I'm really sorry for getting you wrapped up in this," I said softly. "And I'm sorry about the way I acted in the Jeep."

"It's okay."

I tried to avoid her eyes, but something about her gaze held me.

"Your moneyman—Gary—told me he thought you were after revenge," she said. "He thinks that's the only thing that could make you act the way you do. He said you were an unfeeling man."

"Big mouth," I muttered.

"And he's got the broken nose to prove it," she reminded me.

I cringed inwardly, thinking of how I'd last seen Gary in the Polaroid photo—eyes closed with a knife sticking out of his chest. I decided not to tell Cass about it. She'd been through enough.

She was too observant.

"What happened to him?" she asked.

"He was the informant you so astutely mentioned earlier," I replied.

Her eyes widened. "Did you…?"

I shook my head.

"Not me. I have a bad temper," I said with a shrug. "But not *that* bad."

"But he's not okay," Cass persisted.

"No," I admitted, and I couldn't keep the disgust out of my voice. "I think Monato felt he'd served his purpose."

"It bothers you?"

"People aren't disposable, Cass. I don't like what Gary did. But I like what Monato did even less."

She was examining my face carefully, as if searching for honesty, and I shrugged again.

"In my line of work, it's helpful to have a temper. More often than not anyway," I told her. "I am not going to bother faking an apology for mine, either. But contrary to apparently popular belief, that doesn't mean I'm unfeeling in other regards."

She went quiet for a minute, and I worried our entire stay at the cabin was going to be like that—long silences punctuated by awkward conversation.

"Do *you* think I'm unfeeling?" I asked.

"There's some scotch in the cabinet," she offered.

Her lack of response to my question made me uneasy.

"I don't want any," I told her with transparent irritability.

"I was telling you for selfish reasons." She bit back a grin. "And no, I don't think you're unfeeling. But you made it clear you don't like it when I call you a hero."

"You want scotch?" I responded, pretending not to have heard the rest, even though it lifted my spirits.

"Just to take the sting out."

She pointed to her neck and I winced. Somehow, I'd managed to momentarily forget about the zip cord that had been tied around her throat. The mark was fading to an angry purple already, but I winced at the thought it might leave a scar.

Something else that's my fault.

My hands clenched into fists, and I fought to relax my fingers, one by one.

Cass cleared her throat, and I jumped up to search the cabinet. I found it on the top shelf and I knew right away it was a good bottle. I opened it and sniffed it appreciatively—it was an aromatic single malt, and the scent was enticing as I poured it. Sighing, I grabbed a second glass and pulled two neat shots. Cass drank hers back quickly and held it out for a second before I even took a sip of my first.

"Much better than the acetaminophen Billy left for me in the suitcase," she said.

I poured her another, then sealed the bottle back up. Cass's eyes were already bright by the time I got back to the futon.

"You look…happy," I teased.

"Drink yours," she replied. "You'll look happy, too."

I laughed. "I'm really more of an *angry* drinker. But you should've guessed that."

"I don't believe it, actually," she said. "Sit."

She pulled back the quilt and patted the spot beside her. I raised an eyebrow deliberately and slowly, and Cass giggled. I liked this easygoing side of her as much as I liked the quiet but straightforward one.

"So you're not going to sit?" she asked. "You'd rather stand there staring at me?"

I rolled my eyes and joined her. I stretched my legs out and pretended not to notice as her thigh brushed mine. I took a sip of the scotch, savouring the flavour in my mouth.

"Are you about to get angry again?" Cass teased.

"Maybe."

She grabbed my drink and took an exaggerated sip.

"You wanna tell me what it is you're so mad about?" she wondered out loud.

"No."

She made a ridiculous pouty face that reminded me of the convincing role she'd been playing at the warehouse. My eyes focused automatically on her lips, and the immediate memory of the way they felt pressed against mine made me very conscious of how close she was sitting to me. Cass smiled and winked, and her expression gave away the fact that she was playing it up on purpose.

I sighed and pushed down a sudden urge to pin her to the futon. I moved away and she moved closer again.

"Does alcohol always have this effect on you?" I asked.

"Yes. No."

I narrowed my eyes at her.

"I've only had one drink. And a bit. Although…I do feel a bit funny," she confessed.

"You said Billy gave you acetaminophen, right?"

"I thought it was. I have the bottle here. Somewhere."

She reached down to the floor, and her T-shirt slid up, exposing the smooth skin on the small of her back. I ached to lean over and run my fingers along it. I had to grip my knees tightly to stop myself from doing it. Cass righted herself and grinned at me with a flushed face. She handed me an unmarked, white pill bottle and I grimaced as I opened it.

"These aren't just acetaminophen," I informed her. "These are prescription acetaminophen. With codeine."

Her arm was still draped across my lap, and I tried unsuccessfully to disentangle myself from her. She sighed and buried her head against my chest. I could smell my shampoo in her hair, and knowing she'd used it did nothing to ease my increasingly apparent desire.

"This is nice," Cass said softly.

"Nice," I agreed in a thick voice.

She turned her face toward me, and I found myself staring into her slate-coloured eyes. Her pupils were big, her skin was pink, and when she parted her lips to speak again, I had to look away in order to control myself.

"John?"

"I had a brother," I said through gritted teeth. "Colin. He died. He was killed, actually."

Cass sat up and I exhaled with relief, mingled with regret.

"Who did it?" she asked.

I decided impulsively to take a chance.

"I don't know. Maybe Monato. Maybe someone else in the game. My little brother was in the same line of work as me," I explained. "He looked up to me, wanted to be like me in every way he shouldn't have been. He born when I was eight, and after my parents died, he became my responsibility."

"I get it," she said. "Siblings have to stick together."

Cass was still watching me, and her face was full

of understanding. What could she possibly understand about my violent world? Nothing. But I nodded anyway.

"I tried to keep him out of it," I told her. "I actually moved him away from this city for a while, just to avoid getting him involved. But as soon as an opportunity came up to come back, he jumped on it, of course. I pretended I was okay with it, and I tried to help him from where I was. He knew Billy, too, so I had him keep tabs on Colin when he could. But with the kind of work we do…I had to move back."

"I understand," Cass told me softly, and she sounded like she meant it.

"He was busy with work, but I *knew* something was wrong the last few times I talked to him," I admitted. "Although it wasn't until our very last conversation I realized he was putting himself in danger. He was investigating something that had nothing to do with him, nothing to do with work. I told him to leave it alone, but he was stubborn. I was out of town, and even though I got out here as fast as I could, I was still too late."

I stopped for a second as a fresh surge of guilt and pain coursed through my body. My throat felt thick, and I was grateful when Cass handed me the last of her scotch.

"If I'd been twelve hours earlier, I might've been able to stop it," I told her. "But by the time I arrived home, they'd already cleaned house. His boss was dead. His girlfriend was dead. *Colin* was dead. No one was talking because *they* didn't want to wind up dead, too."

I closed my eyes. It was so hard to think of how one decision I'd made had changed the course of my life. It was impossible to not blame myself. And I remembered it like it was yesterday. I had flown in—why had I decided it was a good weekend to go away?—only to be greeted by Billy at the airport. The second I had seen his face, I'd known I was too late.

"So when you got home, you did what? Took over so you could figure out who did it?" Cass wanted to know, and I sensed she might be trying to steer me to a less painful conversation.

"Yes," I replied gratefully. "I forced my way in right in the middle of the chaos. I knew the business—I was doing it before Colin was an adult. I knew Billy, and he vouched for me. I came in with my family money and picked up the pieces quickly. God knows I had the motivation."

"And no one knew Colin was your brother?"

I shook my head. "Nobody except Billy. To everyone else, he was just some guy in the wrong place at the wrong time. As far as I know, nobody except the man who killed him knew much more than his name. If that."

Cass put her head on my shoulder, and I took a shaky breath, enjoying the way she made me feel. It was glad, too, to have explained myself, and to have shared a part of it with her I couldn't really discuss with anyone else.

"John…"

"Yeah?"

"Colin was a mercenary, wasn't he? That's why you hate them?"

I drew in an involuntarily sharp breath.

"Yes," I admitted. "He was."

"It's okay," Cass told me in a sincere but sleepy

voice, and patted my hand gently.

"Thank you," I said.

She didn't answer, and after a minute, I realized she'd fallen asleep. I wrapped my arms around her, carried her to the bedroom, and tucked her into the big, wrought iron bed. I kissed her gently on the forehead, and decided to try and get some sleep myself.

Chapter Twenty-Five

In my mind's eye, I saw the cold, starkly white room of the morgue.

No! I tried to scream at myself. *Don't go in!*

I knew I had to be unconscious, and I begged myself to wake up. I didn't want to relive what was on the other side of that big, silver door. But I couldn't stop the memory/dream from moving forward.

Blair had her hand on my shoulder.

Where was Dean?

Blair wondered, too, and said so.

I shook my head at her. Blair and Dean and Jeannette hadn't overlapped in the real world. They were more like different chapters in the book of life that made up *me*. Jeannette had been before. Dean had come after. And Blair was my now.

I tried to make myself say that to the dream-Blair, but she was just waiting for me to answer, a quizzical look affixed on her face.

I don't know, I saw myself mouth.

Blair frowned her displeasure and pushed the door open.

I stared at the body down on the table, and it was surreal both in that moment and in my memory.

You two are enough alike to be twins, people always said to us.

And there she was, eyes closed and peaceful,

looking just like me. I wanted to touch her, but I didn't let myself.

It's her.

The coroner—if that's what she was—nodded at me and covered my sister's face with a finality that made me burst into tears.

Blair touched my shoulder again. I wanted to shrug her away. She wasn't supposed to be there. She *hadn't* been there. No one had. But her hand stayed, forcing me to turn and face her.

It will be okay, Cass, I saw my friend tell me. *She was so unhappy.*

Was she? I asked.

Yes, of course she was.

The drinking. The men. The moodiness. I could remember when it had started—I could almost pinpoint it even, though I never understood why it had happened the way it did.

"Drink a bit, smoke a bit, live a lot," my sister used to tease.

I wished she'd been able to take her own advice. Maybe she would have stayed happy.

I'd turned around for a second as Blair tried to lead me out, and that's when I saw the tattoo. The sheet fell away from her upper body, exposing her shoulder. Small and black, laced with green. A tiny snake. It happened the same way in real life, too. And I wanted to examine it closely. To commit it memory.

I pulled away from Blair and walked over to my sister's body.

How funny, I said. *I never knew she had this.*

Then Blair dragged me outside, where it was raining.

I woke up crying. I wasn't sure what I'd been dreaming about, but my mind went instantly to John.

John's brother, I concluded. *Colin.*

The pain he tried to hide as he told me about his brother's murder made me hurt, too. I knew that kind of pain, and it made it easier for me to understand his anger, and his inability to see himself as a hero.

When I put my hand up to my face, I could feel wet tears there. I exhaled softly, and even in the dark, I saw my breath. I pulled the blanket up to my chin and rolled over. I tried to go back to sleep, but whatever sadness I had experienced in my dream lingered.

Sighing, I got up and padded over to the bedroom door with the blanket still wrapped around my body. I looked out, and saw the fire was burning low. John was lying on the upright futon, and I gazed at the outline of his body for just a moment, admiring him. He was unmoving, except for the rise and fall of his chest.

"You asleep?" I whispered.

His answer was immediate. "No."

I stepped over to the futon and sat—almost but not quite—on his feet.

"You worried?" I asked.

"Not any more than usual," John replied, and I could hear the smile in his voice.

"It's cold in my room," I told him.

"Do you need another blanket?"

"I'd rather just sit here with you for a minute," I admitted.

"All right," John said, sounding pleased. "Are *you* worried?"

"Surprisingly…not much."

John chuckled. "What is it you do in your other life

that makes you laugh in the face of death?"

I grinned. "I work with deaf and hard-of-hearing children. I teach sign language."

"Sounds terrifying," John joked.

"Well…Not so much," I said. "But that must make *you* happy, since it means your analysis of me was so close to true."

"What analysis is that?" he asked.

"Your complete breakdown of my life and personality. The one you made on the day you kidnapped slash saved me," I reminded him. "Satisfying but low-paying job, remember?"

"Ah, yes. Anything else I was right about?" he wanted to know.

"Some," I admitted. "My mom passed away when I was young, and my father disappeared shortly after that. I *am* quiet, mostly. And reserved. At least I am now. I like to think that I'm smart…Or at least that I've smartened up."

"And your heart?" John asked in a quietly teasing voice. "Did some bad man break it?"

"You're the only bad man I know," I replied lightly.

He laughed. "Is that right?"

"Besides," I added, "It wasn't a man who broke my heart anyway. It was a woman."

"Oh?"

"Not like that," I said quickly. "My sister died suddenly six years ago."

I paused after I spoke the words, and closed my eyes. The memory was still so painful. John placed his hand on my knee and squeezed reassuringly.

"Do you want to talk about it?" he asked.

"No."

"Okay," John said easily. "Why don't you tell me what you'd be doing right now if you were at home?"

"Sleeping," I replied immediately. "Isn't it, like, three in the morning?"

"More like four," John corrected.

He smiled at me, and for the first time ever, in the soft glow of the firelight with this big, dangerous man, I *did* want to talk about Jeanette.

"She was my half-sister, and my best friend," I told him abruptly. "My mom had her when she was only sixteen, and we were nine years apart. Jeanette was the coolest person in the world. She never treated me like the pain in the ass little sister I'm sure I was. When she was nineteen and I was ten, our mom died of cancer. My dad couldn't handle it. He took off, and left me with my sister. For five years it was all right most of the time, and great at some moments. We shared a studio apartment in the city. She was a waitress, and an office assistant, and even a dog groomer at one point."

I smiled at the memory of her coming home, covered in dog hair and soap, and telling me that at least the dogs didn't complain about the way she served their kibble.

"It's funny isn't it? How you took care of your brother, and my sister took care of me...But somehow I just can't picture you cutting doggy toenails," I said to John.

He grinned. "I've done worse jobs."

"I'll bet," I replied, and took a breath before continuing in a soft voice. "But when I was fifteen, Jeanette died, too, and I was alone."

John squeezed my leg again, and I fought back the

tears that were coming. I didn't want to tell him the whole story, not because I didn't trust him with it, but because it was just too hard for me to talk about it. I did it anyway.

"She was so full of life," I said. "I know you hear that about people sometimes, but with Jeanette it was really true. She was thankful for every bit of money that came in. She bought me a cake for each A I brought home from school. Everything was a celebration for her. Then one day it just…wasn't. She went away for the weekend and left me with some friends. When she came home, she was depressed. She never said what happened—maybe she thought I was too young to understand whatever it was. Then she was gone *every* weekend. And then for a week at a time. And even when she was home, it was like she wasn't really there."

I stopped for a minute and closed my eyes. It was hard to explain the change that happened. Harder still, because I had never understood it. She'd gone from a fun, vibrant individual to a tormented soul in what seemed like moments. I'd tried so hard to keep her in the world with me, and I had failed.

I swallowed thickly and moved on.

"She ODed on something. Cocaine? Heroine? I don't even know. The police told me later it probably wasn't accidental. Without Jeanette, my life was empty. I went crazy, trying to live without her. I kept expecting to wake up and find her there, you know? So I ran away. For six months, I was completely on my own. I squatted in a few apartments. I slept in shelters, or on the street. Anything to keep me out of foster care. I celebrated my sixteenth birthday between two garbage bins behind a fast food restaurant."

I stopped again, thinking about it. I couldn't even picture myself doing any of those things. But back then, I slept in places I wouldn't even walk through now.

"Social services caught up to me just after I turned sixteen, and they bounced me from foster home to foster home. I don't think they knew what to do with me. I didn't drink or cause trouble. But I wouldn't talk to the shrink they sent me to, either. I was trying to grieve, and no one would let me," I said. "They finally placed me in a group home. Then I met Dean Sternlight. I thought we were alike. His family was alive, but they had been useless at raising kids. He was in the system for a long time, and he'd been bounced around, too. I didn't know it then, but it was mostly because he was ripping off his foster parents. Some people won't report it, you know? They think they're doing the kids a favour by not turning them in. And Dean was…charismatic. Charming. And God awful manipulative. He was older, and working as a volunteer for the group home."

John had an irritated scowl on his face, and it made me smile a little. As much as he claimed not to be a hero, he was clearly interested in protecting me.

"Go on," he told me in a growl.

"He treated me all right," I said, and John's face got even darker. "Or at least he was content to let me just *be* instead of trying to force me to deal with my issues. It was such a relief. When I was almost eighteen, Dean proposed, and it seemed to make sense."

"Is that right?" John asked too quietly.

I brushed off his expression with a shrug.

"You've looked into my financials, so you already

know how it turned out," I told him. "Two months in I knew it was a mistake, even though I hadn't found out yet about the credit cards or the loans. Three years had gone by since I'd lost my sister, and I was ready to start the healing process. But I stuck with him anyway. I kept telling myself I wasn't going to be like my dad and just run out when the going got tough. A whole year of married life went by, and I thought things weren't so bad. Then the creditors started calling. Our car was repossessed. We had to move to a terrible apartment in a crappy part of town, and Dean couldn't keep a job. We separated after that. It took me two whole years to get the annulment finalized, and another to really start getting past it. That was what I was working on when you… found me. I was celebrating the first anniversary of my freedom."

"I can't picture it," John said. "You don't seem like the type to let herself be taken advantage of."

"I'm not," I replied. "Not anymore. Dean had been fine for the sad, brokenhearted Cass. But the Cass who was ready to move on and grow up—the rebuilt me— could never love a man like him."

"Who *could* the rebuilt you love?" John asked softly.

The air in the room changed.

John's hand was still on my calf, and he sat up without taking it off. He slid it up gently until it was just above my knee.

I looked over at him, and the blanket he'd been using slipped down, revealing his bare chest. The tattoos on his arms spiralled across his shoulders and torso. I noticed again how the images blended together with the lettering. The word *EYE* twisted to form a delicate, gray iris and a blacker than black pupil gazed out at me. The letters that formed the word *OCEAN* were sprawled in lazy, circling waves. The mix was overwhelming and heady.

"They're poems," John breathed as he followed my stare.

"Poems?"

He nodded almost imperceptibly. His hand was on my thigh now, and I could feel the pulse in his thumb, thrumming against my skin. The steady beat of it was almost as distracting as the nearness of his face to mine.

How did he get so close, so fast?

"It's a whole book of poetry," John murmured.

His lips were inches from my own, and I was torn between watching them move and soaking in the intensity of his gaze.

I leaned back against the futon, and he shifted so that one of his legs was pressed between mine

"What kind of poetry?" I asked, trying to make myself focus on anything other than the feel of his body against me.

He moved his hand from my thigh to my waist, and slid it up my side. I tingled in response, and my breathing quickened. His fingers trailed up the underside of my arm, forcing it above my head. He pinned it there, and stared down at me.

"They're my words," John said, "My poems."

His admission just about undid me.

"John." His name came out as an incomprehensible mumble.

Dear God.

His lips came down, hovering just above mine.

His phone rang. I willed him not to answer it.

It rang again, sounding more insistent, and he groaned regretfully.

"I'm sorry," he said, and peeled himself away from me to grab the phone from the table.

"Seever," he greeted. "Hi, Billy. Shitty timing."

I watched his face darken.

"Fine. No."

He paused again, then grabbed his jeans from the floor. He slipped them over his hips.

"Yes, we'll be ready."

John turned back to me with a mixed expression on his face—partly apologetic, partly amused. And very annoyed.

"Billy found Monato holed up at one of his trashy apartments," he told me. "I'm going after him before we lose him again."

"What about me?"

"Billy will be here in twenty minutes. He'll take you somewhere safe."

"Again?"

John nodded. "Let's get packing."

He turned away, and whatever moment we'd had was lost.

Chapter Twenty-Six

I was sure Billy wasn't happy about my request, but as we loaded into the two cars, I was utterly certain it was the best option. It wasn't because Blair's parents' cabin wasn't safe—it was just that I was paranoid about its remoteness. If something happened to me and Billy, it could be days before Cass realized, and who knows how long after that before she might be able to get ahold of someone to take her off the mountain. Sure, Blair knew where her friend was, but as far as she was concerned, Cass was on a romantic getaway and in no hurry to get back.

Besides that, if the wrong person got to Cass first…

So far Monato had been a little too good at finding us, and the thought of hiding Cass somewhere she couldn't get away from scared me. I had to assume that Monato had more than one set of eyes on me. My track record for keeping her safe wasn't good. The hotel was compromised. So was the warehouse. It was safe to assume my private apartment was being watched, too.

No. She needs to be somewhere no one would think to look.

I wanted her somewhere with better-than-spotty cell service, somewhere she could easily escape from.

And somewhere I can access her, I admitted to myself.

So. The house was it. Only Billy and I knew about its existence. Even the neighbours on the street had no idea who lived there. The electric bill was in my dad's name, there was a landline, and it was so completely un-*John Seever* that it was practically a safe house.

I didn't know how long it was going to take me to chase down Monato, and I wanted Cass to be hidden. But accessible.

"It's the best option," I muttered again.

Billy shook his head, but he didn't argue. Cass just looked concerned, and I smiled at the sight of her furrowed brow.

"Hey," I said. "When this is done, I'll come right to you. I won't even stop to gloat."

"I'm worried," she admitted.

"Oh, so *now* you're worried?" I teased.

"I can tell from your face you are, too," she told me.

I kissed her cheek so I wouldn't have to tell her a lie. I helped her into the car and closed the door carefully before turning to Billy.

"Take her the back way off the mountain," I commanded.

Billy grumbled something about the suspension in the sedan and priorities. I put my hand on his arm, and he looked up at me in surprise as I spoke again.

"Please," I near-pleaded. "Don't let anyone see you. I'm not going to be shy about driving through the city, and I'd prefer it if all eyes were on me rather than on her."

"All right," Billy agreed gruffly, and stepped into the driver's seat.

I waited until they were out of sight before I

climbed into my Jeep, thankful I had it rather than my boat of a car. I had no interest in making a grand entrance, and I wouldn't stand a chance of making a subtle one with the Parisienne. I had a feeling Monato might be expecting me anyway.

I got into the vehicle and began a slow descent off the mountain. The sun was just barely visible on the horizon, and I was conflicted. I was in no hurry to confront Monato, but I wanted this part of my life to be over. I'd been chasing Colin's ghost for what seemed like a lifetime. When I'd upped and run to come after him I had nothing to hold me back. Our parents were long gone. I wasn't married, and had no intention of becoming attached at any time. And I owed it to my brother. He followed in my footsteps and had died as a result.

I'd happily and forcibly transferred my skills to business with Billy, and strong arming my way in had been surprisingly simple. My associates likely sensed I'd had nothing to lose. My fearlessness had led to controlled recklessness and an absolute ownership of my role there. None of them questioned my motivation—no one even knew about my family ties to Colin. He'd been low down on the rungs, but I was an instant celebrity. There was no reason to connect us. So I'd been able to stalk his murderer without fear of interference, and I'd been able to carry on with the finance end of my business with no problems as well.

But Cass wanted to know the why for everything. She pursued my motivations and made me question them by pervading every corner of my mind.

I tapped the steering wheel in time with the steady hum of my thoughts of her.

I could still smell her light scent on my own body—not quite perfume, not quite sweat. Just *her*. And the remembered feel of her soft skin underneath my hands made me shift uncomfortably in my seat. But it was more than that, even. I loved the look of my ring on her finger. It was beautiful there, and I was secretly pleased she had been leaving it on, even in private.

Did it matter, if I never found my brother's murderer? I had never considered it to be otherwise. *If I could have a life with Cass...maybe it didn't. Or at least it could matter less.*

I smiled to myself as I made the last turn off the mountain. I would do what needed to be done with Monato, and then I would pursue Cass with a vengeance. I was pretty sure it wouldn't take much to seduce her—or maybe that was a wishful assumption— but I was suddenly very sure I wanted something more than that. I wanted my ring to stay on her finger. Permanently.

I glanced at my watch. I'd been on the road for over an hour already, and forty-five minutes more would put me at the city limits. I slowed down, considering what my options were. I wasn't sure exactly how my impromptu meeting with Monato was going to go, but I *was* sure it wasn't going to be either smooth, or pleasant.

Chapter Twenty-Seven

As Billy pulled the car into the upper-class, typical suburban neighbourhood, I had to fight to hide my surprise. The tense exchange between him and John hadn't had me thinking of ultra-cliché white picket fences and large, cookie-cutter homes. Billy had a deep frown etched into his forehead, but he was still driving through the neighbourhood with easy familiarity. I couldn't help but wonder how much time a man like him could possibly spend in an area like this one. I opened my mouth to ask him.

"You don't like me," I stated instead.

I hadn't meant to say those words, but as soon as I had, I realized it was probably true. I'd spent the last few days thinking it was the other way around—that I didn't care for the gruff-voiced man, that there was just something about *him* that bothered *me*.

"Why?" I asked.

Billy sighed. "I'd like to say it's not you personally, but that'd be a lie."

My heart sagged. I guess I half-hoped he'd deny it.

"Why?" I asked again.

"You know that big red rock on your finger?"

He nodded toward my hand and I blushed. I supposed I could have taken it off when we weren't in public, but there was something comforting about wearing it.

"It was John's grandmother's ring. He's been holding onto it since he was twelve years old, waiting for the right girl," Billy told me.

I waited for more, but he just slowed down the car as we pulled into a large cul-de-sac and eased it into one of the long driveways at the end.

"Wait here," he said in his usual gruff voice.

As I watched him get out and key in the code for the garage, I twirled the ring on my finger self-consciously. If what Billy had said was true, why would John share that kind of information with him? After all, he hadn't told me the ruby was a family heirloom. Irrational jealousy clouded my brain for a second, and try as I might, I couldn't push it aside.

Billy hopped back into the car and guided it into the garage. When he turned off the ignition, he put his hand on the back of my seat and turned to face me. His gaze was serious.

"John and I were associates before he ever came to work in this part of the business. We've been working together for a long time. I might even say if we were different men, we'd be friends. And I have never seen him lose his focus. Not once. But all of sudden he's forgetting meetings. He's hiding out. In fact, I'd say he's not really conducting business at all," Billy told me.

"And you think it's because of me?"

"I *know* it is," Billy corrected. "And I'm worried about him. I should be out there with him, right now. Not here babysitting you. When this deal with you is done…"

As he trailed off, I wanted to point out to him that I'd been thrust into John's world against my will, and to list off all the things I'd been planning on doing with my week-long vacation. I couldn't, and I could see from the look on Billy's face that he was genuinely concerned about John. I couldn't fault him for that. I looked down at my lap guiltily.

"I'm sorry," I said.

"Are you doing it on purpose?" he replied.

"No."

The older man laughed, and the wide scar on his face bent around his amused grin.

"I don't *want* to dislike you," he admitted. "And in spite of your obvious ability to distract John…For whatever reason you seem to put him in a good mood."

"This has been him in a *good* mood?" I asked.

Billy laughed again, before his face went serious. "I don't think I've seen him smile so much since Colin died."

"Thanks," I said gratefully.

"Don't thank me yet," Billy suggested. "I'm about to give you a reason to hate me back."

I smiled a little before I realized he wasn't kidding.

"What now?" I wanted to know.

"I'm going to feed you, and I'm going to lock you in John's bedroom," he told me.

"Why? Where are you going?"

"To help John."

I sighed again, and resigned myself to being held captive once more.

Chapter Twenty-Eight

I parked at the end of Monato's block and got out of my car. I rolled my eyes at what I saw. The apartment building where Monato was rumoured to be holed up was flanked by four cars with tinted windows. I could see three armed guards blocking the front entryway.

Does he think I'm bringing an army?

I shook my head. The man was all flash and fire and no finesse. If our roles had been reversed, he probably *would* have brought an army.

I watched from a distance. One of the sedan's doors swung open and two more guys rolled out. One of them reached back into the car and dragged out an angry young woman. Even from my vantage point, I could see her ferocious expression. She took a few steps toward Monato's building, then tripped and yelled something unintelligible at the guards. The two men laughed and one of them gave her a nudge with his foot. I gritted my teeth, but she just got up and shoved him. She straightened her ridiculously short skirt and tried to walk away, but stumbled once again as one of her high-heeled shoes snapped. One of the thugs put out his arm to steady her and she pushed it away irritably. She bent down, yanked the heels off completely, and stomped into the apartment building. She was drunk or high or both.

"See something you like?"

I spun around with my fist in the air, and Monato stepped back just in time.

"I didn't think she'd be your type, Seever. I don't know why, but I thought you preferred blondes," the other man said mockingly.

"I like my women sober and willing, Monato," I retorted.

His face darkened. "I think you like women who don't belong to you."

I snorted. "You may have that backwards. And where are your men?"

"I think we can settle this like grown-ups," he replied. "Don't you?"

"You mean you don't want them to see you have your ass handed to you?" I asked.

"Hardly." Monato said.

I hesitated. He was expecting me to come at him. He probably thought he'd robbed me of my connection to Leo, and the income that went along with it. He'd come into my club, into my hotel, and he'd tried to take Cass from me, too. I was fed up, and had a right to be.

I want nothing more than to crush you like a bug.

But instead of speaking my mind, I just smiled tightly. He thought Cass was dead.

"How much do you want for her?" I asked.

Monato frowned. "For that waste-case of a brunette?"

I rolled my eyes. I doubted he even knew her name.

"How much for Cass? For my wife," I clarified.

"I think I already…" The other man trailed off as he caught the dead serious expression on my face.

"You think you already what? Took her out of the equation? I guess you're not as efficient as you think you are."

Monato snorted derisively, and I pulled my phone out of my pocket.

"Have a look," I suggested. "Check out the time stamp."

I'd taken the picture the previous night, not long after we'd arrived at the cabin. Cass was looking up at the mountain with a small smile on her face. Monato scrutinized the photo with pretended indifference. Even if it hadn't had the date and time at the bottom, the marks on her neck were clearly visible. Monato shoved the phone back at me.

"So what? You want to…*buy* her from me now?" he sounded utterly disbelieving.

I nodded. "Yes."

He tilted his head quizzically to one side. "But if she's your wife, then she's not one of my girls. And that means I can't sell her to you."

"Monato, I'm giving you an out," I said as patiently as I could manage. "I'll pay you whatever the going rate is. Hell, I'll double it. Tell people you pulled one over on me. It gives you an excuse to leave her alone—maybe it even justifies your claim on her, I don't know."

"And it gets you what you want, of course," Monato added.

"Yes," I agreed. "It does."

He tapped his chin with exaggerated thought. "These decisions aren't entirely up to me."

I sighed tiredly. "What do you mean, Monato? They're your girls, your decisions."

He looked uncertain for one second, and I wondered what he was playing at. I just wanted to pay him off and be done with it, everything else be damned. I'd already made up my mind to tell Cass what I'd done, and let her choose whether to stay or go.

God, I hope she stays. My heart twisted when I considered that she might not.

Monato's snide mask was back in place.

"Did you know a man named Colin, by any chance?" he asked innocently. "Minor player in the game before you came along."

I went very still and answered in a carefully neutral voice. "I knew him."

Monato smiled. "I thought you might. Something about you reminds me of him. Not the way you look, exactly. More something in your demeanour."

I gritted my teeth and said nothing. Monato's smile widened.

"He was interested in a girl, too," he told me. "What was her name? I'm so bad at remembering them."

"I don't know."

"Was it Marion, maybe?"

I felt my face pale. Billy had a daughter about Colin's age. But she had become involved with the wrong people, and had died of an overdose—right around the time my brother was killed. I remembered one of the last conversations I'd had with him. I'd been trying to talk him out of staying in the business any longer. I thought he'd been trying to change the subject.

"I met a girl," my brother interrupted my rant about the dangers of carrying on.

"You didn't," I argued.

"But I did."

"Tell me about her," I replied with a sigh.

"Soon," he told me. "We just have to sort out a few things."

With his job the way it was, what other kind of girl would he have been exposed to? But it never occurred to me that she was someone I already knew—someone who had become entrapped in Monato's little harem with no way out.

"Mary-Anne," I corrected, knowing it was true.

"That's right. Mary-Anne. Colin offered me a deal eerily similar to the one you're trying to make."

"Mary-Anne was Billy's daughter," I stated.

Monato's smile slipped just a little, and I realized he might not have known.

"That's right," I said. "That girl, who you hooked on drugs and dragged into your so-called *business* was my colleague's kid."

"Mary-Anne was a whore and an addict, like the rest of them," Monato replied.

"She was barely eighteen," I replied angrily. "You manipulated her into becoming something she wasn't. And you wouldn't let her go when she asked to be set free."

"That's a little more simplistic than I see it," Monato countered with a shrug. "But Colin saw it the same way. He accused me of the same things—more even. Trust me when I tell you that all these girls are the same, in the end. What is with you guys and your hero complexes?"

"Shut up."

"I tried to talk him out of it," Monato continued. "But he was stubborn, like you. At least he was until I shot him."

His confession should have thrilled me, or at least offered some kind of satisfaction. It's what I'd been after for six months. But all I felt was rage mixed with despair. For several seconds it almost crippled me. The smile on Monato's face set my teeth on edge. And he must have been laughing it up, knowing.

I let the anger crash through me as I lunged at Monato. He easily sidestepped my anger-fueled attack. I stumbled, and the other man reached for his gun. I went for my own, knowing he had already taken the advantage. He cocked his pistol as I fumbled to draw mine.

He went down, crumpling to the ground with a comically surprised look on his face. His eyes rolled back in his head as he hit the ground with a thud.

"You don't fight well when you're mad," Billy said in his gruff voice.

He was holding a short, black baton, and smiling grimly. He reached back and swung again, even though Monato hadn't moved an inch. Blood was already pooling behind his head.

"I think you got him," I said.

"Just making sure."

"He killed Colin," I told him.

"I heard."

"And he as he as much as killed Mary-Anne, too," I added. "Did you know they were involved?"

"None of my business." Billy shrugged in a way that made me think he *had* known.

"Why didn't you tell me?" I wondered out loud.

"I'm just trying to make my peace. Didn't figure you needed any more heartache."

"You're a better man than I am, then," I replied. "You'd think it would make me feel at least a bit better, knowing for sure. Closure or whatever. But I don't. I feel…empty. And still angry."

"I'm no less pissed, either," Billy said. "It's been six long months for both of us. I'm sad. And mad. And this douche bag facilitated my daughter's death. And none of that is going to disappear in one instant."

I lost my cool for just a second.

"Then what the hell is the point of revenge?!" I yelled.

Billy chuckled at my outburst and kicked Monato's still body.

"I'll let you know if I figure that out before you do," he said.

"Thanks," I replied with just a touch of sarcasm.

The older man put his hand on my shoulder.

"You've got a girl locked in your room," he reminded me gently.

The dark cloud hanging over my heart lifted marginally.

Cass.

I glanced down at Monato.

"You'll do what needs to be done with him?" I asked.

Billy nodded, and his smile was sinister. "With pleasure."

Chapter Twenty-Nine

Billy left, and he hadn't come back in what seemed like hours.

I rattled the door handle again, knowing what I'd find. Locked from the outside.

Maybe it really *was* hours since the older man had left. Since I had no watch and there was no clock anywhere to be seen, I didn't have a way of actually knowing. What would Blair do in my situation?

Probably broken a window and climbed out, I chuckled wryly.

I was better at waiting than she was. But even I had my limits. I'd flipped through a classic car magazine, a men's health magazine, and I was on my third go through a cooking magazine. I tossed it down with a sigh. Who keeps three-year-old magazines in their bedroom anyway?

Everything in the room seemed to have a layer of dust on it, actually. The big black armchair where I'd been sitting was stiff and unused, and I'd had to wipe it down before settling in. But the decor wasn't really without personality. The walls were gray, and the dresser and bed frame were stained antique black. One corner had a nook cut into it, and instead of a computer station, it housed a mahogany desk, the chair where I sat, and an empty bookshelf. An electric fireplace completed the cozy corner, and I wondered what kind of reading material John would put there if he used it with any regularity. Not the magazines, I hoped.

I stood up and walked around. It was a big room.

Nearly as big as my studio apartment.

A framed map of the world took up most of one wall, and a huge flat screen TV dominated another.

I went over to the dresser and pulled the top drawer open. *Boxer briefs.* I closed it again quickly and examined the framed photo on top instead. I picked it up and wiped away the dust. A younger John and a little boy holding a huge fish grinned at the camera. They had the same mischievous twinkle in their eyes and matching buzz cuts.

"That's Colin," said a tired voice from behind me.

I spun around. John was watching me with a pained smile on his face.

"My parents had a cabin in the Rockies. We went every year."

"He looked like you quite a bit," I told him.

He took the frame from my hand and used his dress shirt to wipe away the rest of the grime.

"I should take better care of this," John said softly. "And the house, too."

"Do you live here?" I asked.

"I used to."

I looked at his face. He seemed different. Quieter. More reserved.

"What's wrong?" I wanted to know.

"We got Monato," John said. "He's no longer a threat."

"So you… took care of him?"

"Billy's disposing of him right now."

I tried to assess my feelings about that statement.

Logically, I knew I should've been horrified, but all I felt was relief.

"That's good, right?"

He shrugged and traced his fingers along my hand. My heartbeat quickened. He paused at the borrowed ruby ring.

"It means *our* business is done, too," he told me.

He threaded his fingers through mine and a rush of warmth spread through my body.

"John," I said, and my voice sounded a bit strangled.

He slid his hand out of mine, set the picture back on the dresser, and grasped me by both my elbows. He pulled me slightly closer, and my world shifted. I forgot about the photo, and Monato, and our business deal. I put my hands on his hips and dragged him toward me before pressing myself against him. The contact made me gasp.

John placed one hand on the side of my face and the other on the small of my back.

"I'd like to kiss you, this time without the excuse of our little act," he said in a soft voice.

I tipped my head up in acquiescence, and he brought his lips crashing down on mine. He paused to look me in the eye, and I saw passion, and warmth, and an indescribable safety there.

It emboldened me, and I slid my fingers to his shirt and began unbuttoning. My gaze fixed on his tattooed chest. I admired the fluidity of the words and images, drinking in their appeal. I pushed his shirt down, and moved to kiss the inked illustrations. My lips burned pleasantly as they traced the art that decorated his body.

John let his arms fall to his sides and groaned low

in his throat.

I unbuckled his belt and slid it out of his pants. I tugged a little hesitantly on the top button, and blushed when it popped open easily.

"Cass," he murmured, and lifted me up and carried me over to the king sized bed.

He placed me carefully on top of the pillows and I sneezed at the dust that flew up. John laughed, and I blushed.

"So beautiful, even while sneezing," he teased.

He kissed me again, this time until I was nearly breathless, then he rolled me over so that I was sitting on top of him.

"I've been waiting forever to do this," he said in a thick voice as he looked up at me.

I smiled.

"Me, too. Forever," I admitted, and it felt true.

But had it even been more than seventy-two hours? I didn't even know what day it was anymore.

I lifted my arms up, and he tugged my shirt off impatiently. As he tossed it aside, I leaned down to kiss him again. He trailed his hand along my waist and up to my back. We rolled over again, and his chest was pressed against my torso. I sighed as he swept my hair away from my neck and trailed gentle kisses along my back, working his way slowly from one shoulder to the other.

He drew in a sharp breath and stopped. I waited for him to start again, or to speak, but he just lay there, very still.

"John?" I said hesitantly. "Are you okay?"

"What the hell is this, Cass?" he demanded in a fiercely angry voice.

"What?"

"Move," he commanded.

"Move where?"

"Away from me. This is my bed, and I want you out of it."

I jumped up and covered my chest with my arms. I turned to face him. His body was rigid, and his eyes were flashing. He glared at me for one second and then deliberately turned on to his back.

"Get out," he said to the ceiling.

"John?"

"Get. Out."

I grabbed at my shirt and tried to yank it away, but it was stuck under John's shoulder. He made no move to help me. He was still staring straight up. I pulled harder, and my face began to burn with embarrassment. I choked back a sob. I tugged once more, and with a suddenness that made me stumble, my shirt finally came free.

I shoved my head and arms through it, and looked pleadingly at John. He ignored me. I slipped my boots on, and took a step toward the door.

"Cass?"

My heart jumped.

"Yes?" I replied hopefully.

"Billy should be back by now. He'll take you wherever you want to go. You'll probably find him in the guest room downstairs."

I flung the door open and ran down the hall without looking back.

Chapter Thirty

When she left, I pretended not to hear her. She was crying, and it made my chest hurt. I rolled over, and willed the pain there to stop.

I pulled the memory of the tattoo—Monato's mark—to the front of my mind. I pictured it on Cass's shoulder, permanently etched into her otherwise perfect skin. It angered me. No. It *infuriated* me.

No wonder Monato had wanted her so badly. Before all of this, had she been his in more than one sense of the word? The thought burned my ego. I felt used, too. I might've been willing to protect her if she'd just told me.

Maybe.

But she said didn't know *Monato,* argued a small voice in the back of my head. *She seemed scared.*

Or she's a very good liar, I countered.

I rolled off the bed and yanked my jeans on angrily.

Either way, let him have her.

I opened my night stand drawer and pulled out a bottle of single malt and my favourite snifter. I looked at them both, put the snifter back, and took a swig from the bottle.

Part of me thought I was being unreasonable. An even bigger part of me thought I should be chasing after Cass, begging her to forgive me. So what if she had been a part of Monato's group of girls at one point? She clearly didn't want to be there now. She really was afraid of the man, I was sure of it. And maybe she hadn't even been a willing participant. God knows I got the impression some of his girls hadn't been.

But why didn't she just tell me? I took another large gulp of whiskey.

I answered myself again. *Because she was manipulating you.*

That made perfect sense, too. I'd been trying to get to Colin's killer for six months and if I'd been Monato, I'd have wanted me watched as I got closer to the truth. I hadn't managed to plant anyone in Monato's crew, but all he'd had to do was send a pretty face my way and that was it. How simple? Why hadn't I thought of it?

Mostly because I would never want to expose a woman—any woman, not just Cass—to that life, I admitted to myself.

I'd seen Billy's daughter lose herself in that world. My own brother had been murdered as a result of Monato and his views on women.

But Cass...

Why would she get the tattoo that marked her as one of his if she wasn't?

I cracked my knuckles angrily as I focused on the evidence in front of me. There was an answer I wasn't seeing. But the whiskey was making my mind feel slippery. I was missing something.

I drank again. And again.

I wanted out. I was done. I'd found Colin's killer, and I had no reason to keep doing what I was doing. It was time to go back to my other life. I grabbed my phone and prepared myself to make the call, excusing myself from the business. I dialled and took another angry swig of whiskey. The bottle was getting empty, but I didn't feel any better. In fact, I felt worse.

"Hello?" a deep voice on the end of the line said.

But something was nagging at me.

"Hello?" the deep voice said again.

"Never mind." I replied, and I hung up.

I walked out of my room and down the hall to Colin's room. I hadn't been inside in who knows how long. Since before Colin had come into the business. Since before we had moved—three years earlier—out of the house and into separate apartments in the city. I took a big sip of my whiskey, opened the door, and stopped.

I frowned into the room, trying to figure out what it was that gave me pause.

It was too *clean.*

There should have been thick dust everywhere, like there was all over my room, like there was all over the rest of the house. But there was just the thinnest layer, as if someone had been using it much more recently than three years ago.

Had Colin been in here not long before he died? I wasn't sure..

I walked over to the nightstand and slid it open. A leather holster and a gun were lying inside. I was sure they were Colin's, and I was doubly sure he hadn't owned them when we were living together.

"Why had he come here, of all places to conduct his business?" I muttered to myself.

I answered my own question. *For the same reason* you *did—because no one else knew about the house.*

So he'd been working in secret. On what?

I went over to his closet and shoved aside his suits, exposing a hidden panel on the wall. When he was a teenager, he'd stashed everything there—Playboy magazines, beer, his drawing-filled journal. If he really had been working on something, it would be in there.

I pulled the panel off, dragged out a medium-sized box, and took the lid off. My hands were shaking a little as I took the file folder out from inside. I tried unsuccessfully to steady them. As I opened it, the pictures inside fell onto the floor.

There were three small stacks, each with three photos a piece, and each with an index card of information written in illegible shorthand. It was Colin's writing, and I felt a pang as I looked at it.

I spread the three stacks out and bent down over them. The images of three dead women's shoulders—marked exactly the same way Cass's was—made me angry and nauseous once again.

Monato's mark.

But the pictures also made me curious.

I slammed the bottle down beside the paperwork and shoved thoughts of Monato and Cass aside.

I lifted the stacks, and moved the top photos away so I could examine the next ones. They were of the same women, only these ones were full body shots. I picked them up, one by one.

The first one was Billy's daughter. I recognized her immediately. In life she'd been a petite blonde with an easy smile—not much more than a kid. In the picture, she was thin to the point of illness, with protruding shoulder blades and a gaunt face. She'd had a drug problem, and it was evident in the images as well.

I glanced at my brother's notes and I read the index

card. *Front, M. Overdose.*

I couldn't imagine how hard it must have been for him to keep this information about the woman he loved.

There was a date recorded on the card, too, and I winced as I realized she had died only two weeks before Colin.

Why had he kept these in here?

I moved on to the next stack of pictures. They were of another blonde with a bruised face.

Cross, B. Overdose.

Colin had phoned me after this girl died. He'd been the one to find her. I closed my eyes and remembered the conversation.

"Why are you calling me?" I had asked. "I thought your new work meant severing all ties."

"C'mon, John," he whined. "I've got a job to do."

I sighed. "Fine."

It had been two months since I'd spoken to him, but I caved anyway. I always did with Colin. With everyone else, I could lay down the law. But never with him. He was only twenty-one—eight years younger than I was—and could bend me to his will at any given moment.

"I had to do something I didn't like today, bro," he said.

"I have to do something I don't like every day," I had laughed.

"I found a body," he whispered.

I stopped laughing. "Did you call the cops?"

I wasn't sure which answer I wanted. A yes would mean he'd endangered himself. A no would mean he was that much closer to stepping over the edge. He didn't respond to my question directly anyway.

"Here's the thing, one of the older guys found a girl, too. Just like this one. In the same apartment, but years ago" Colin told me. "So I'm doing some digging."

I felt instantly worried.

"You shouldn't be talking about it," I said.

"It's hard to not talk to the guy who's helping you clean up a body."

"Stay out of it," I commanded. "You get paid to carry a gun and clean up messes, not to worry about how the messes got there."

"I don't think I can do that, bro."

"These girls…they get in over their heads and they wind up dead," I stated with false casualness.

"Not all of them want to be where they are," my brother replied coldly.

Why hadn't I picked up on that? He had probably been talking about Mary-Anne, and I had just dismissed it.

"Colin, you said yourself you've got a job to do," I had reminded him.

"This is bigger."

He sounded excited and that worried me more.

"I'm on my way home," I told him. "I'll cover your ass when I get there."

"No!" he protested. "The whole point of this was to separate ourselves. It was even your idea."

"Sort of," I muttered.

But I hadn't wanted to tell him that our then-mutual boss had pushed for the move and I had fought against it. Colin had been told that the whole thing was my idea, and that had made him so damned proud.

I put down the picture of Cross, B., and moved on

to the third photo. It was an older, more blurry picture, and I was sure she was the other girl Colin had mentioned, the one who had been found in the same apartment. How did he manage to acquire it?

Canter, J.M. Overdose. (Suspected suicide.)

I stared down at Canter's face, and my world halted. It was a jarring stop, and for a second, my whole world was still.

It was Cass's face there, eyes closed peacefully. The same high cheekbones. The same full mouth and delicate nose. Yes, this girl's hair was dark. But when I looked closely, I could clearly see lighter roots as her scalp.

"Jesus," I swore.

I cursed my own stupidity.

It had been *Cass* getting a tattoo at Yun's, not her friend, I realized. That ink on her back had been fresh. She had been commemorating this woman—her half-sister. Jeanette. She had as much as told me so at the cabin. But I'd had no reason to make the connection.

Except you should have, said that small, irritating voice in my head. *And you probably would have, too, if you weren't so intent on getting her to pretend to be your wife.*

I had sent her away with no questions, with no explanation.

"I'm an idiot," I muttered.

I fumbled around for my phone. I wondered if Billy had already dropped her off at home. I hoped not. I dialled him quickly and he answered on the first ring.

"Things not going as planned, Casanova?" He sounded tired.

"Not exactly," I admitted. "I'm a fool. A jerky

fool."

Billy laughed. "No shit."

"You on the road?" I asked.

"Nah. Been back awhile. Didn't want to disturb you."

Dammit.

"Do you think she'll forgive me?" I wanted to know.

"Who?"

"Cass. Who else?"

Billy paused. "Forgive you for what? Isn't she up there with you?"

"I told her to leave," I replied.

"For God's sake. Why?"

"I made a big mistake," I said. "I thought she was one of Monato's girls."

"What?!" I'd never heard the man sound so surprised.

"I said it was a big one."

Billy was silent.

"And I told her you'd give her a ride wherever she wanted to go," I said. "She didn't ask you?"

"I didn't see her," Billy told me quietly. "I've been asleep in the guest room for hours."

Chapter Thirty-One

I couldn't shake the kicked-in-the-gut feeling. I'd left the house without seeking out Billy. Maybe he would've driven me, but I had been too busy trying not to cry to be able to ask. And it was probably the best thing anyway. If he *had* taken me anywhere else, I would've felt like too much of a personal connection had been made.

Not that I was kidding myself. They could find me if they really wanted to. But I just wanted to be alone with my thoughts.

And now that I was…I was regretting it.

I had dragged myself onto the bus that would take me right to Blair's house, and found a seat. But she lived on the opposite side of the city, and as house after house blinked by through the bus windows, the trip was even longer than usual. It gave me too much time to dwell.

I'd just barely managed to begin to clean the slate of the sorrow I'd felt about losing Jeanette, and now it was all dirty again, this time with the hurt of rejection. Why did it cut me in so similar a way? I'd been young when she died, and I was probably already a mess waiting to happen. Her death had just been the thing to push me over the edge.

This isn't the same, I told myself.

But it made me hurt in such a similar way.

You'll get over it, I told myself harshly.

I was sure it was true. Or pretty sure anyway. It had taken years for me to get over losing my sister. But she had raised me. It had even taken me years to get over Dean, and I hadn't loved him, not really. Or at least, I hadn't felt the same passion as I had when I was with— I cut myself off and I gave myself a mental kick in the rear end. We'd only had three days together, and it had been for business purposes.

But for some reason it was like a lifetime had passed.

The bus finally made its wheezing stop a few houses down from Blair's place. I thanked the driver in a forcedly bright voice and took a breath. My friend was going to be pissed at me. And she had a right to be.

But I need her. It was selfish, but I walked quickly to her door anyway.

I knocked hesitantly, knowing she was already mad, and knowing she'd be even madder when she heard the scanty details I was willing to share. I'd already decided I would keep my promise of relative silence. I wouldn't tell her about the money John had offered me. I wouldn't tell her about his questionable career choices, or about exactly what had happened with Monato. But she was still my best friend.

I knocked again, and she still didn't answer. Had she seen me through the window and chosen not to come to the door? I resisted an urge to call her name loudly. The upstairs neighbour was a cranky, eighty-year-old man who wouldn't appreciate the disturbance after eight o'clock in the evening.

I glanced into my purse. I had seen it sitting by John's front door and grabbed it. I dug through it until I found my cell phone. Dead, of course.

And even if it wasn't...Blair might not have answered my call anyway, I admitted.

Tears welled up again and I fought them back.

"I need you to forgive me, Blair. Quickly," I said up into the air.

A hand on my shoulder made me jump and spin around. My friend's grumpy neighbour glared at me. He was dressed in mismatched plaid pajamas and brown slippers.

"Sorry, Mr. Reimer," I said automatically.

"Don't think she's here," he grumbled. "Lots of ruckus about an hour ago. Been quiet since then, though."

"What kind of a ruckus?" I asked.

"Shouting. Heard a crash. Thought maybe she was fighting with a boyfriend."

An immediate chill made me shiver.

"She doesn't have a boyfriend," I stated.

I turned and banged on the door.

"Blair!" I yelled, and I could hear the frightened edge in my own voice.

There was still no response.

"Blair!" I shouted again.

"Did you try the handle?" Mr. Reimer asked.

"What?"

The old man rolled his eyes and reached for the doorknob. When he turned it and pushed, the door swung open easily.

"Easy peasy. Need anything else? No? I'm going back to bed," Mr. Reimer told me.

I waited until he'd disappeared around the side of the house, then took a breath. I stepped into my friend's suite.

"Blair?" I called a little more quietly, and not honestly expecting an answer.

The state of the living room made me feel sick to my stomach.

Blair's favourite antique lamp had been knocked to the ground, and the light bulb was in pieces. Her wooden rocking chair was on its side. A glass carafe was shattered on the coffee table, and orange juice was spread out in a sticky mess across the carpet. Blair's keys, purse and cell phone were sitting in a pile on the sofa. A crumpled hand towel was wedged between the seats.

I reached down and picked up the towel. Even before I got it close to my face, the familiar and nauseating smell of ether hit me.

"Oh no," I whispered.

My thoughts tumbled quickly through my head.

This is my fault.

But Monato is dead!

Should I call the police?

And then a sharp blow to the back of my head cut me off.

Chapter Thirty-Two

I'm not a calm man by any stretch. Usually my outbursts of emotion are limited to angry ones, and almost always directed at people who deserve it. In my opinion.

But what I was feeling about losing Cass was entirely different than that. My gut was clenched and my heart wasn't obeying any kind of normal rhythm pattern. I couldn't push it aside, and I didn't have an outlet. *But it was Monato who was fixated on her,* I reasoned. *And he's gone.*

I growled at the calm, reasonable conclusion.

"She deserves to know about her sister."

I didn't even realize I'd spoke out loud until Billy answered.

"She doesn't need to know," he said.

"What did you find out?" I asked.

I'd sent him out to see if he could follow her.

"That driving around a neighbourhood full of block parents is not the safest way for me to garner information. Oh, and most of your neighbours thought you'd died," Billy said.

"That's not helpful," I growled.

"Once she realized I wasn't a crazy stalker, the nice lady at the end of the block gave me some cookies and told me she'd seen a sad-looking blonde girl at the bus stop. You're just lucky she's a sucker for a good love story."

I felt so relieved—for just a moment—that I ignored his snide comment.

"I'd want to know, if it was my sister," I stated.

"Cass is *not* you," Billy replied.

"I think I'm having an anxiety attack," I muttered as I paced through my living room.

I stopped in front of the coffee table and ran my fingers so hard through my short hair that it actually hurt.

"Why won't she answer her damned phone?" I wondered out loud for the fifth or sixth time.

Of course, I couldn't call her anymore anyway because about ten minutes earlier, while I'd been waiting for Billy to get back, I'd tossed my cell phone across the room. It had landed in my half-full whiskey snifter. I gave it another dirty look.

I knew it was better to drink it out of the bottle.

"John, you told her to leave. You didn't even give her a reason," Billy said patiently.

I spun to face him. He was shaking his head at my antics.

"Do you really expect her to answer your call? Would you?" he asked. "She's probably hurt. Give her a day or two. Maybe even a week."

"I can't, dammit."

"You're gonna have to."

"I don't want to. I feel like I have to tell her."

I sat down on the couch and put my head in my hands.

"You need to consider that this might be over," Billy told me.

"I have," I replied. "I'm trying to talk myself into

believing it."

"Are you sure you're not trying to talk yourself into believing the opposite?" he asked. "To give yourself an excuse to go after Cass?"

"Dammit! Yes, I've thought about that, too."

It was a real possibility. Just because I'd been so fixated on knowing what had happened to Colin didn't mean it was the same for Cass. She'd already accepted her sister's death. Why did I want open up that wound for her?

I sighed loudly and looked up at Billy.

"Fine," I said in a deflated voice. "The job is done."

He nodded.

A phone rang then, from inside my coat. I stared at the jacket, hanging on the back of a chair, and wondered what the hell was going on. Billy reached into the coat pocket and pulled out an old flip phone. He tossed it to me, and I caught it reflexively.

It rang again in my hands, and I stared stupidly at the blocked number for a long moment before answering.

"What?" I said.

"Mr. Seever?"

"What?" I said again.

"I believe you were looking to speak with me?"

"Who is this?"

I wasn't in the mood for games.

"This is Vance's boss."

"Vance who?"

There was a pause.

"Vance who?" I repeated.

I was getting ready to hang up.

"The tattoo artist."

My mind finally made the connection. This was the phone he had left in my car after our meeting.

"You're too late," I responded. "I found him, and I took care of him."

"If you're speaking about Monato, I'm afraid you've only taken care of half of the problem," said Vance's boss.

I frowned. "In what way?"

The man on the other end of the phone sighed loudly. "As he told you, quite some time ago, a man came to us with a specific request. He wanted Vance to tattoo several women with a small snake. I believe you know the one. It's black with green eyes and it's wrapped around a thorn-spotted branch."

My heart thudded unevenly. "And?"

"And the man who brought me the girls was a man named Monato."

"You're about twelve hours late," I snapped. "I figured this out myself."

"Monato was *not* the man who commissioned the art itself," Vance explained patiently. "The man who requested this specific tattoo did so over the phone. This man never did give a name."

"Why are you telling me this?"

"Vance was quite insistent that I contact you. He told me he learned that at least three of the nine women I have tattooed have met with unfortunate circumstances," the man said. "I don't like to see my art end in this way."

My heart sank. I had sent Cass packing, and possibly endangered her life. A cold sweat broke out on my forehead in response to that thought.

I forced myself to speak calmly. "And?"

"And I heard, also, that you had eliminated Monato. I wanted to make sure you had all of the information you needed."

"Monato killed my brother," I said thickly.

"I'm aware," Vance's boss told me calmly. "But—"

I cut him off. "Now that he's been *eliminated*, I don't care who else was involved with the tattooed hookers."

"All right."

The other man hung up and I turned to Billy.

"What now?" he said.

"It wasn't him."

"Who?"

"Monato."

"Monato's the one who killed your brother," Billy reminded me. "He pulled the trigger. He admitted it."

I looked up at him and nodded. "Yes. But what if he wasn't the one who aimed the gun?"

I leaned toward the coffee table with the intention of grabbing my keys, but Billy was faster.

"You're drunk," he stated.

"I'm fine," I lied.

"You've been drinking since before I woke up. Probably started even before that."

Billy sighed at my desperate expression.

I narrowed my eyes at him. "You know where she is, don't you?"

"I was asleep when she left."

"My neighbour told you something else, didn't she?" I asked. "About where Cass's bus was going?"

"She mentioned the Uptown 5 route," he replied.

"And you know where she was going," I pushed.

"I wish I didn't," the older man grumbled.

I gripped his arm.

"Listen," I said. "I'm not going to make her do anything she doesn't want to. I'm not even going to ask her to come back and stay with me. I just have to warn her that Monato wasn't working alone. Please."

Billy sighed at my desperate expression.

"She's going to Blair's house, I'm pretty sure. I'll take you," he offered a little reluctantly. "But if Cass isn't there, we're leaving. And if she *is* there, but doesn't want to see you, we're leaving. Once you've said your piece and she doesn't explicitly ask you to stay..."

"I get it," I muttered. "We're leaving."

Billy shook the keys emphatically, and I followed him out to my garage.

Chapter Thirty-Three

I came to with an aching head. I was bound, gagged, and blindfolded.

Shit, was my first thought, and my second was, *How many times in a week can one girl get kidnapped? This is getting ridiculous.*

Then panic set in like a reflex.

I screamed as long and hard as I could against the fabric in my mouth. All that came out was thick sound that didn't carry past my own body. I inhaled deeply through my nose and tried again. It was at least as ineffective, and it made me choke and cough, too. I wanted to try a third time.

But I might throw up if I do.

The futility of my situation made me want to pound my fists against something. But of course, they were tied behind my back, and I was stuck in a chair.

I tried to spit out the gag. I used my tongue to push on it, and my teeth to loosen it. The effort made me sweat, and after a minute or less, my whole mouth ached.

But it's looser, I told myself as I took a rest. *It really is.*

I tried to focus my other senses on my surroundings. The air smelled damp, and if my efforts hadn't made me heat up, I probably would've actually found it quite cool.

A basement? Or a cellar?

I went back to work on the gag. It *was* giving way, at least a bit. I chewed harder on the cloth, and it split open suddenly.

"Ha!" I said triumphantly.

My voice echoed a bit, and I decided I must be somewhere bigger than a cellar. A low groan came from somewhere else in the room, and I froze. The groan came again.

"Hello?" I called quietly.

For a second, there was no response.

"Ugh." It was a croaked reply, but definitely a human one.

"Who's there?" I whispered.

"I don't feel so hot."

I gasped at the sound of the familiar voice. "Blair?!"

"Cass?" she groaned. "Where the fuck are we?"

A hysterical giggle escaped my lips. "Oh, thank God. You're alive."

"Sort of alive," my friend corrected. "But I've got a very bad taste in my mouth. And my head fees like it's stuffed with fluff."

"Ether," I muttered.

"Huh?"

"That's how I felt after I got dosed with it at the club," I explained, then frowned.

But Monato is dead.

"You got ethered? I thought someone slipped something in your drink."

I sighed. "I wasn't being entirely honest."

"No shit."

"I'm sorry, Blair."

"That you lied? Or that you got me kidnapped?" my friend asked.

"Both," I replied. "But John told me he killed the guy who drugged me."

"He did what?!"

"I just don't understand who's kidnapped us if Monato is dead," I said, ignoring my friend's shock.

"Well, maybe—no scratch that—*hopefully* your new boyfriend lied about killing him," Blair replied. "And I'm not even sure which is worse."

I frowned even harder, thinking of John's face as he confessed that the creepy man had been taken care of. His expression had been tired. Maybe just a touch satisfied. And more than a bit regretful. But nothing about his demeanour had made me think he was being deceptive.

"John was telling the truth," I told my friend. "I'm sure of it."

"So then whoever kidnapped us…He and John are what? In cahoots?" Blair asked.

I laughed. I couldn't help it. I tried to imagine John describing his relationship with his business associates as being "in cahoots." I laughed harder.

"I've missed you," I said between giggles.

"Save the lovey-dovey crap for when we've escaped," Blair suggested. "Or for your kidnapper boyfriend."

I sobered up immediately.

"This wasn't him," I insisted.

"You can't be sure of anything. And if the Monato guy is dead…" She trailed off and I could hear the doubt in her voice.

"I know," I replied. "I don't get it either. But I'm

sure John wouldn't bother kidnapping me."

My friend drew in a breath, and I knew she wasn't going to let it go.

"But—"

I cut her off, and my face went red as I spoke. "If John wanted me, he could've had me, Blair. He wouldn't have needed to kidnap me."

My friend made a sudden and gleeful noise. I rolled my eyes. Leave it to her to be in the most terrifying situation of her life and yet *still* find a reason to squeal like a teenaged groupie.

"I knew it," she said. "I heard it in your voice from the beginning!"

"Forget it," I replied. "He made it clear he wanted me gone."

Tears pricked my eyes as I said the words. There was some shuffling from Blair's corner, and suddenly her hands were on my knees and her face was pressed against mine.

"Are you blindfolded?" she asked, and yanked the cloth down.

"Blair!" I yelled.

"Are you sure he meant it?" she asked.

"Blair!" I repeated even more loudly. "You're not tied up!"

"You are?" She sounded puzzled.

"I'm not sitting in this chair for my health," I told her.

"He probably didn't really mean it," she said.

"Why aren't you tied up?" I muttered.

"They probably thought I was dead."

"Why would they think that?"

"Well... They did shoot me. By accident, I think."

"What?!"

"When I was halfway passed out," she explained. "I heard the shot and some screaming. I swear, they only hit my ear. But there might've been some blood."

My stomach churned. "My God."

"I'm fine," she insisted.

"You're not…Never mind. Blair…Untie me!"

She started yanking on the ropes, chattering about men and their mixed messages. I gritted my teeth and ignored her as I ran through the facts of our situation. I wasn't naive enough to believe our kidnapping was a coincidence. And in spite of John's angry dismissal, I really didn't believe he'd been lying about Monato's death. He had no reason to.

"And he wouldn't have let me leave—not like that—if he thought I was still in danger," I muttered out loud.

Blair paused in her rambling. "Why *did* he kick you out?"

"I don't know. We were…involved," I said with a red face. "And then…"

"And then what?"

I frowned. "And then I think he saw my tattoo."

"So what? He hated it?" Blair asked.

"I don't know."

"That doesn't make any sense," my friend said. "I saw his arms. He's covered in them."

I agreed, but I didn't really have any other explanation.

"You're free, by the way," Blair announced.

I stretched my arms and my legs and breathed a big sigh of relief. I glanced around the room. It was dark, windowless, and had a packed-dirt floor. It was hard to see, but I guessed it wasn't a basement. At least not one under a house.

"Where *are* we?" I wondered out loud.

"I don't know," Blair replied. "But I see some stairs. And a door. So I say let's go!"

Chapter Thirty-Four

Cass's friend Blair lived in one of the older residential neighbourhoods in the city. It was full of charming old homes that had been converted into apartments, and as Billy drove through it, I surveyed the area critically. It was not as safe-looking as I wanted it to be.

"You're not just gonna see her," Billy finally said.

"I'm not looking for her," I muttered.

"Bullshit."

"I was just thinking about what a crappy neighbourhood this is," I said.

Billy gave me a look that let me know he didn't believe me at all.

I tapped my fingers on my knee. The steady stream of alcohol I'd been consuming all day was starting to wear off a little, and the result was the beginnings of a headache and an enhanced feeling of desperation.

"What did I do, Billy?"

The other man shook his head. "Which part are you talking about? I've got a list."

"All of it!" I yelled without meaning to.

"What were you expecting?"

"I don't know," I admitted in a weak voice. "I brought a normal, everyday girl into this mess of a life I've got going on...I just need to know she's safe, all right?"

"All right," Billy agreed, and he pulled the car up in front of one the old houses.

"Will you wait here?" I asked him. "I promise to control myself."

The other man nodded curtly. "Ten minutes."

"Unless she wants me to stay," I said hopefully as I let myself out.

I pretended not to hear his groan as I slammed the door shut. My spirits dropped and my anxiety lifted more than marginally as I went around the side of the house. The basement door was wide open, and I frowned.

"Cass?" I called, and then added, "Blair?"

There was no answer.

I took a cautious step forward, and the hair on the back of my neck stood up. I was suddenly wishing I'd brought my weapon.

"Dammit," I said as the cool metal of a gun barrel pressed down on my back.

"Unbelievable."

I was so surprised by the authoritative tone in the familiar voice that I almost spun around.

"Don't move," the voice commanded. "Where's Billy?"

"Doc?"

"Don't sound so surprised," he said. "It's just plain insulting."

"Where's Cass?" I countered.

"What *is* with you and that girl?" the other man asked.

I shrugged and he sighed.

"Billy's around the front, boss…" The voice trailed off as the speaker caught sight of me with the gun pressed between my shoulder blades.

"Thank you, Gary."

"Yeah, thanks," I added sarcastically.

I got a solid shot to the kidneys for my efforts, and I had to force myself to remain upright. I looked up and met my former accountant's eyes.

"You're alive."

"And kicking," he replied.

"Well. That's one less death I'm responsible for," I said.

"Your girlfriend—no, wait, it was wife, right? She's alive, too. She'll stay that way as long as you're behaving," he told me.

"Fine," I agreed quickly.

There was long pause and the Doc laughed. "I've been thinking of you as impervious to feeling for so long I really expected you to just tell me to go ahead and kill her."

I didn't answer.

"Gary has a phone here. You're going to use it to text Billy. Tell him you've reconciled with the girl and you'll make your own way home later," the Doc instructed. "And be convincing."

I typed the message.

Using Blair's phone. All is good. Staying with Cass. Call later.

I handed the cell back to Gary, who nodded and pressed send.

"Sorry about this," the Doc said, then cracked me on the head with the butt of the gun.

Chapter Thirty-Five

It was drizzling outside, and just past dusk, making it hard to see. But after just a few minutes of walking through the area, I knew where we were anyway. The big, familiar buildings and the dirt road identified it as the block of warehouses where I'd almost been killed the day before. My limbs shook, and I gripped Blair's arm for support. She held me steady, and when she flicked her hair back, I saw that she had the tiniest nick on the top of her ear. She brushed off my concern.

"We'll get a bandage later. Right now… Let's figure out how to get home. I take it you recognize this place?" she asked.

I nodded, not fully trusting myself to speak.

"Do you think there's a phone anywhere?" my friend asked. "We need to call the police."

"No police," I gasped.

I slumped against the exterior of one of the buildings, and stayed there with my head in my hands. Water was seeping from the wall through to my clothes and it made me shiver. It also reminded me that I was still wearing the clothes John had provided. I felt guilty. I'd glanced at the tags. The pants alone cost more than my monthly rent.

"Hey, Cass? You'd better get a grip."

I looked up through blurred eyes, and realized I was crying.

"Sorry," I said immediately.

My friend shook her head. "No, it's okay. I mean, cry over the guy. Just do it later, because someone's coming."

She was right. I could hear the sound of heavy feet squishing through the packed dirt.

"Too late," Blair murmured as a group of men came around the corner.

She grabbed my arm and we hugged the wall as they went by, oblivious to our presence. I stared at them as they approached, and tried not to breathe.

One was a heavyset man who could've been Yuri the mercenary—or the warehouse guard who looked just like him—and the other was a gangly, familiar man in a jean jacket. His nose was covered in white bandages. It was definitely Gary, the money man.

But what really caught my attention was the person they were dragging between them.

It was John, I was sure of it. Even in the near darkness, I could see the poetic tattoos scrawled up and down his arms. His head was down and his body was limp. The unnatural way his feet scraped along through the mud made me cringe.

I yanked my friend even closer to the building and tried to melt into it.

Please don't let them see us, I prayed.

They got closer. They paused a few feet away from us, I could make out the smug look on the Gary's face, as well as the blank one on Yuri's.

"Where does Ramirez want him, Gary?" Yuri asked. "All these fucking buildings look the same."

"That's why they're numbered, dumbass," Gary replied.

"You and your goddamned numbers," Yuri muttered.

Gary's face scrunched up, and for a second I thought they were going to drop John and start to fight.

Then Yuri sighed. "Let's just get him where the boss wants him. I'm starving."

"What else is new?" Gary replied, but this time the jibe sounded good-natured.

They started to move again, and as I watched their retreating backs, desperation crept in.

"Okay," Blair breathed. "Now we really have to call the cops."

I gave her an apologetic look. "I'm so sorry. I can't."

"What the hell, Cass?"

"I know it sounds crazy," I said. "But I can't let the police get John."

"Even if we put aside the fact that the man tossed you away like yesterday's lunch, why would they *want* him? He's the victim here," Blair replied.

I shook my head. "Right now he is. But his business isn't legal. At least I assume it's mostly not. And I just can't…"

She stared at me. "You *do* sound crazy, you realize that, right?"

"If I ask you to leave, will you?" I wanted to know.

My friend looked like she was going to protest, but she just she sighed heavily. "How do you expect me to get out of here?"

I smiled weakly and reached into my purse. "You know how you got your license, and you've always wanted a motorcycle but could never afford one?"

Blair's eyes lit up, and I exhaled with relief.

When my friend slipped away on the Ultralow with a solemn vow to *not* call the police, I had a moment of panic.

What are you doing? my inner self demanded. *He's a self-proclaimed dangerous man. He's a criminal. You've been holding his hand like you were on a first date, and now you're going to do what? Rescue him from a bunch more criminals? God knows what these other men are capable of.*

I cursed at my cautious brain, dismissed its ramblings and went off in the direction that Yuri and Gary had disappeared. I rounded a corner and stared forlornly, wondering how I would find John in this sea of nearly identical buildings.

But I didn't have to go far.

A meaty hand grabbed my arm, and my cautious brain cursed me back for not listening.

Chapter Thirty-Six

I groaned as I waded my way back to consciousness.

"Yeah. That's gonna leave a mark."

I squinted up at Ramirez's words. The man was looking at me with a small smile on his face. There was a cruel glint in his eyes, and I found myself wondering how I could have been so mistaken about his personality.

"You've been manipulating Monato this whole time," I stated.

"Among other things."

I felt a small amount of vindication because at least I hadn't been outplayed by that glorified pimp. Monato had been a puppet. A ludicrous, dangerous, and nearly farcical figurehead.

"Where's Cass?" I asked automatically.

"She'll be here shortly," the Doc told me.

And as if on cue, the door swung open and Yuri shoved Cass through.

"Her friend is gone. And is therefore obviously smarter than this one," the big mercenary announced.

"I thought the friend was dead." The Doc sounded confused, but not particularly angry.

"Apparently…We missed."

"They got out of the basement?" the Doc asked. "I'm impressed."

Yuri nodded as he shoved Cass toward me, then pushed her down on to her knees.

"I'm sorry," Cass whispered, and my chest burned with guilt.

It should've been *me* apologizing to *her*. I had treated her badly, and she was still the one being kind. It made me feel even worse.

"Might as well tie them together," Ramirez told Gary.

I ignored my former money man as he bound us together.

"Why didn't you go with Blair?" I asked.

Cass gave me another apologetic look.

It's because of me. The expression on her face— part adoration, part nervous regret—confirmed it.

"I'm fine, Cass," I said angrily. "You should've gone with her. You don't owe me anything."

Hurt flashed through her eyes before she buried it with resolve.

"Do you want us to go after the other girl?" Yuri asked the Doc.

"No!" Cass gasped. "She's not going to do anything. I made her swear she wouldn't call the police."

"You really think I'm going to take that risk?" the Doc asked. "I'm done with loose ends."

"Please," Cass begged.

The Doc sighed and waved his gun around with exaggerated patience. "Help me here first, Yuri. Then you and Gary can get the other girl."

He handed the weapon to the big man, who pointed it at us and waited for the Doc's signal.

I reached for Cass's hand. She resisted for one

second, before her fingers curled through mine, and I squeezed back. Her grip was reassuringly warm, but she was shaking.

"Look at my face," I said, "Not at the gun."

She turned away from the flat black weapon, and met my eyes.

"What are you glad for? Right now," I whispered.

She replied without hesitation. "That I met you."

I smiled, and in spite of my dread about what was going to happen, I felt relief.

"I made a mistake before, telling you to go. I wish I had time to explain it," I said softly. "But in case I never get to say it again, I'm pretty sure I'm falling in love with you."

"You picked a hell of a time to tell me," Cass replied. "But just in case…Me too."

My smile grew into a stupid grin that got even broader when I heard the Doc groan in disgust.

"What a waste," he said. "If Seever had been willing to let go of his brother's death, you two could be having this conversation in the privacy of the bedroom."

His men snickered.

The Doc flicked his hand to the mercenary with the gun trained on us. "Shoot them both, Yuri. Him first, then her. Or the other way around, I don't care."

"What's your plan, Doc?" I asked.

He probably knew I was stalling, but he answered anyway. "Do I need one?"

"You seem like the kind of guy who'd want to brag about it," I stated.

"Fine," Ramirez sighed. "It's a simple one. I placed an anonymous tip to the police about your friend Billy."

I was genuinely puzzled. "Billy?"

"Rumour has it he recently beat a man to death with a baton," the Doc said.

Cass cringed beside me. I made myself ignore it.

"Calling Monato a man…That's a stretch," I replied.

The Doc shrugged. "Doesn't matter anymore. The police will find the baton, either in Billy's apartment or in his car. And when they get to his place, they'll find an incriminating note that will then lead them *here*."

"Then what?" I asked.

"Then they'll find your bodies," Ramirez told me. "And that gun Yuri is holding, wiped clean of prints, but easily traced back to Billy. Nice tidy package."

I let myself smile. "Your plan may backfire still."

"I doubt it." He turned back to Yuri. "Go ahead."

Cass looked like she wanted to close her eyes, but I kept my gaze on her, and willed her to keep them open.

There was a muted pop, and I waited for the pain, but it didn't come.

Cass!

Her expression hadn't change. She looked toward the ground, and when I followed her stare, I saw that a bullet had penetrated the ground just a foot or so from my knee.

I wrapped my arms around Cass, and she collapsed against my chest as I watched the scene unfold before me.

"What the hell?" the Doc said, and stormed toward the man with the gun. "Am I paying you to aim *that* badly?"

When he reached him, Yuri toppled over. The Doc pushed him with one booted foot, and the other man's head rolled sideways. His eyes were open and blank. The Doc's expression went from annoyed to puzzled. He looked at us, and then nervously around the room. He kicked Yuri over again, then turned to Gary, who was already moving to go after the mercenary's abandoned weapon. But as his fingers closed around it, another muted pop sounded through the room, and Gary went down, too.

The Doc reached for it automatically and a third bullet whizzed through the air. He screamed in pain. The gun fell from his hand, and as he flexed his fingers, blood began to seep from his palm.

"I'd hold still if I were you, Ramirez," I suggested calmly.

The other man gave me a cold stare, then bent over to fumble with something in his boot. Blood smeared along his khakis as he brought his hand back up. He held a knife out with a shaky grip, then yelped as a third gunshot cut across the air. The Doc fell forward, and a vibrant red stain spread out across his backside.

I laughed.

"You shot him in the *ass*!" someone yelled.

Chapter Thirty-Seven

Cheers erupted all around me, and it took me more than a few seconds to understand what was happening.

The room was swarming with black-clad police officers. One of them came over and patted John familiarly on the back before untying him. John grinned and started loosening my own bonds.

"Why don't you look worried?" I whispered as he finished. "These are cops. We should run."

"It's fine, Cass," he said.

"It's not," I told him urgently. "When they find out what you do for a living, they're not going to be so nice. I'm so sorry. Blair must've called them."

"I'm pretty sure it wasn't Blair."

"How can you be so sure?"

John gave the ground a guilty-little-boy stare and I narrowed my eyes.

"Are you an…informant?" I asked.

"Not exactly," he replied slowly.

One of the armoured cops came over and handed John a set of handcuffs.

"It's your collar, Seever," the other man said. "Why don't you slap these on Ramirez."

John shrugged without meeting my eyes, and I watched in amazement as he walked casually to the wounded criminal and then expertly attached the cuffs to his wrists.

"Miss?"

It took me a second to realize the uniformed man was talking to me.

"Yeah?" I replied faintly.

"The EMTs are going to take a look at you, make sure you're okay. Then we'll need you to come to the station to give one of us a statement."

"I'm fine."

"You sure?"

I looked up at the fresh-faced policeman and nodded.

"All right. I'll get a detective to collect you for debriefing." He sounded doubtful, but he walked away anyway.

I was lying, of course. But my issue wasn't a physical one.

"John?" I called, and then more loudly. "John!"

I couldn't see him in the crowd, and my knees gave way. I slumped to the ground.

"Hey," said a familiar gruff voice.

"Billy."

I was actually glad to see the scar-faced man, and when he pulled me to my feet, I let myself sag against him in relief.

"John's gonna be a bit busy," he told me. "I'll take you somewhere less crazy."

He led me outside, and when I shied away involuntarily from the noise, the flashing lights, and the dozen or so cop cars that dotted the parking lot, he steered me away from them. I exhaled gratefully when Billy let me into the familiar sedan.

The officers waved him through their roadblock, and Billy guided the car toward the highway.

"You got questions?" he asked after a few minutes of absolute silence.

"I just don't get it," I responded. "Is John an undercover cop?"

"Something like that," Billy snorted. "But more like a rogue agent."

"And you?"

"I'm worse than he is," Billy muttered, then laughed out loud.

I couldn't see the humour in the situation at all. I leaned over and put my head against the cool window.

The gruff man sighed. "I'm just going to let John explain things to you, okay?"

I nodded. "Where is he?"

"At the station by now."

The countryside passed by in a blur, and we were in the city almost too quickly. When we reached the big brick building, I had to force myself to get out of the car on my shaking legs. Billy held my elbow as we went up the steps. I made myself ignore the curious stares of the cops inside. I knew what they saw—a young girl in torn but expensive clothes, covered in dirt, with a tear-streaked face—and I could only imagine what they thought.

Billy brushed past them like they didn't exist. We went down a long hallway, and for a second it seemed as though he was going to put me in an interrogation room, but when he stopped in front of a door and opened it, I saw it was actually just a lounge.

"No one will bother you," the older man assured me. "And I'll make sure John comes right in."

"Okay."

I sat on one of the leather couches and tried to get

comfortable. It was an impossible task. Even if I had been able to sit still—which I couldn't—I wouldn't have been able to keep my mind from examining every detail of the past few days.

The club. Did he really own it?

The hotel?

Why hadn't he just said something? Or put me into protective custody?

I was starting to feel angry now that the adrenaline was leaving my body.

What kind of cop endangers a civilian's life?

The door swung open, and I spun to face him with a furious tirade ready. But as soon as I saw him, the words went out of my mouth.

"You changed your clothes," was all I could manage.

It was irrelevant, but true. He was wearing charcoal gray pants that hugged his hips in a way that made my mouth go dry. I brought my eyes up, pausing to take in his cream-coloured dress shirt, buttoned up to his collar. It fit well, and it was doubly enticing because even though I couldn't see the tattoos through the soft fabric, I *knew* they were there. The memory of my lips pressed against them was enough to make my heartbeat quicken.

I dragged my eyes up to his face, and the pain in his eyes made my throat ache. His face was freshly scrubbed, and even his hair looked like it had been washed. For one second, it made me hyper-conscious of my own sorry state. But his expression was sorrowful, and I pushed down my self-centered thoughts.

"Cass," John said, barely above a whisper, and the sound of my name on his lips in that heartbroken tone undid me.

Without further hesitation, I dove into his arms and pressed my face into his chest. I inhaled. Under the scent of clean clothes and commercial soap, he still smelled of sweat and dirt, and our shared experience in the warehouse.

"Hey," John said softly.

He put his hands on my shoulders and gently pushed me away. I looked up into his brown eyes. Their deep mocha hue caught and held me.

And he still looked sad.

"What's wrong?" I whispered.

He released me and moved away.

"What's wrong?" he repeated disbelievingly. "We both just about died. I've been lying to you since I met you…Please, tell me what's *not* wrong?"

I watched him run his fingers across his head in frustration. I stepped closer and reached up to pull his arms down.

"It's not the worst thing a man has done to me."

It was meant to be a joke, but John's face hardened.

"I don't want to be *that* guy, Cass," he replied angrily.

I sat down on the couch again, waiting for him to blow off his pent up frustration. I felt strangely calm as I watched him explode verbally.

"Goddammit! I shouldn't have interfered with Monato at the club. I should've let you take care of yourself. Or I should've let him keep thinking you were dead. I had an opportunity to keep you safe and I didn't." He finished his rant and looked down at his hands helplessly and finished in a whisper. "I haven't been able to think straight since I spotted you outside of Yun's."

"What?"

John looked at me in surprise—like he had just remembered I was there.

"Outside Yun's?" I prodded.

He looked away guiltily.

"Start from the beginning," I commanded.

"I don't—"

I cut him off. "The very beginning."

He sighed and sat beside me on the couch without letting his knee touch mine.

"Before Colin died—before Monato killed him—I was on the verge of early retirement. I had used my part of our inheritance money to invest in a few hotels, and I was seeing enough return that I didn't *need* to work anymore. Colin was recruited to do an undercover job, straight from training."

"So he went to work as a mercenary?" I asked.

John nodded reluctantly. "I don't blame them for wanting him for the job. He was young. An unknown. And it came naturally to Colin. After all, I'm in law enforcement. Our dad was, too. It made sense to take him and groom him for the role."

"The family business," I stated. "And no one made the connection?"

"No," John replied. "They wouldn't. Publicly, and at work, we used our dad's surname—Friedman. But legally, we were both Seevers, like my mom."

"Okay."

"I told you before he was involved in something over his head," John continued. "And I got here too late. It was *me* who found him in his apartment. I got there first, and I found this."

He reached into his pocket and reluctantly pulled out a piece of paper.

"Before I show it to you," he said hesitantly, "I want you to know I didn't find out about this until after."

I stood up, and reached out to take the paper from him, and froze, mid-grab.

All of the blood drain from my face. I moved back from John unsteadily. He put his hand out to steady me, and I jerked away.

"What is this?" I whispered.

"My brother had it," he told me. "It was shoved into his pocket. I was the only one who thought it was important."

I could see the remembered frustration on his face, and I saw him shake off the residual irritation and focused on my face. I was trembling.

"But…what does it mean?" I asked.

"Do you want to sit down?" he replied.

I shook my head vehemently. "Just tell me."

"The Doc used it as a way to mark his women," John said simply.

"Like a brand?" I sounded as horrified as I felt.

"Like that," he agreed gently.

"But it was on my sister. I saw it."

"I know."

My stomach knotted. My temper flared, and John looked uneasy. I realized it was probably the first time he had seen me get angry. Even when Monato had been after me, and even when he'd kicked me out of his bedroom, I had reacted with relative calmness. I had managed to keep my emotions under control. But

John's revelation made me seethe.

"What do you mean you know?" I demanded.

"I saw the autopsy pictures—"

It was far as he got. I shoved my way past him and out into the hall, ignoring the questioning eyes as I ran through the station.

Chapter Thirty-Eight

I watched her go, feeling helpless.

It wasn't an emotion I was used to, but I was too tired to channel it into one of my more familiar angry outbursts.

I had expected Cass to have a strong reaction. But I had expected her to let me explain, too. As soon as the admission was out of my mouth, her usually kissable lips set into a grim line, and I knew she wasn't going to give me a chance.

Billy came to the door and shook his head at me.

"I told you she didn't want to know," Billy said. "And close your mouth."

He sounded like he was making a joke, but he was frowning, and his scar was bunched up in a frustrated pucker.

"I didn't even get to tell her exactly what happened. Not really," I replied.

"You obviously told her something."

"Nothing good."

"Did you tell you really love her?" he asked.

"No."

"Well that might've been a good place to start." Billy rolled his eyes and punched me in the shoulder. "She can't have gone far. There's about six officers under orders to keep her close."

I stared at him dumbly, cursing my own stupidity.

Of course *I should've started with that.*

"Go!" Billy commanded as he gave me an unceremonious shove.

By the time I hit the stone steps outside, I was running.

"Cass!" I called.

It was dark outside the station, and the rain was pelting down.

"Cass!"

"She's not here," said a wheezing voice.

I glared at the out of breath, uniformed cop who came jogging up the sidewalk.

"Where is she?"

"A car came up and she got in. They took off," he explained apologetically.

Panic made my heart race..

"What do you mean? Tell me exactly what happened…" I squinted at his name tag. "Please, Lieutenant Bosley."

"She wasn't forced into the vehicle, if that's what you're thinking," he replied defensively.

"It was your job to keep her here!" I almost-yelled.

The other cop shrugged. "I called it in, but they told me told me to let her go."

"Who told you?"

He put up his hands. "Dispatch. I just do what I'm ordered to do, man."

I ran my fingers over my short hair. "What kind of car?"

"Big red boat. Nice one, too."

The Parisienne. *Blair.*

"You got keys to a squad car?"

He nodded. "Number eight-oh-five."

"Give them to me."

"No."

"Don't make me pull my gun, Bosley."

For a second I thought he was going to laugh, but when I didn't crack a smile, he relented, and handed me the keys nervously. I smacked him on the back, thanked him, and took off for the parking lot.

I drove quickly with the lights and sirens off. I caught up with them less than ten blocks from the station. When we hit an intersection and the light turned red, I pulled up behind my car and honked unceremoniously.

The driver's side door swung open and I winced as Blair stormed out. She marched to the police car and banged her fist against my window. I opened it.

"What do you want, asshole?" she demanded.

"Cass—"

"No. You can't have her," Blair stated.

She turned and stomped back to the Parisienne. She peeled away without waiting for the light to change to green, and with a sigh, I turned the flashing lights on.

Blair sped up, and I did too.

I ground my teeth together as Cass's friend wove through the streets. I had to force myself to leave the sirens off. It was late, and we were in a residential area, and I didn't really want to draw any more attention from my superiors than I already had.

"Dammit," I muttered as Blair jerked the Parisienne the wrong way up a one way street.

I pulled around the block quickly and drove up the right way. I tensed as the lights of the Parisienne bore down on me. For one very long second, I was sure she was just going to ram straight into the cruiser. I closed my eyes as the tires screeched, and prepared for impact.

"What. The. Hell."

Blair's angry face was glaring at me though my still-open window.

"I need to talk to Cass," I replied calmly.

"And I guess you'd kill us to do it?" Blair yelled.

"It's okay." Cass's soft voice came from behind her friend, and I strained to see her through the dark and the rain.

She took a step forward, and my breath caught a little in my throat. Her hair was wet, and her eyes were sadder than I'd seen them since we met.

"Cass." My voice came out sounding strangled.

You *made her face look like that,* I reminded myself. You *made her feel that way.*

Blair looked from me to Cass, then rolled her eyes.

"Christ," she muttered.

"The uniforms weren't supposed to let you go," I said to Cass.

"I don't think they were too eager to chase me down," she told me.

"I can't think *why* they wouldn't want to get in the middle of this," Blair added.

I ignored her. "Can we go somewhere?"

"In the cop car?" Blair asked, and when I turned to glare at her, she shrugged. "I was just gonna offer to let you guys have the boat. I could drive that thing back to the station."

"No!" Cass and I said at the same time.

"I'll park it," I said.

"All right."

I quickly backed out of the one way road, found a spot and made my way back to Cass and Blair. They were arguing, and I slowed as I approached them.

"You're making the biggest mistake of your life," Blair said.

"Didn't you tell me nothing could top my marrying Dean?" Cass replied.

Blair looked like she was going to say something else, but then she caught sight of me, and gave her friend a shove.

I looked down at Cass. She was smiling a little sadly, and she was getting more soaked by the minute.

"Can we walk?" I asked.

"Yes."

"I live nearby. If you don't want to hear what I have to say, I can call you a cab from there," I offered.

"Don't go in with him," Blair cautioned, and I rolled my eyes.

Cass gave her friend a quick hug, and we left both her and the Parisienne behind. We walked in the rain, not too far apart, but not quite touching. I had to work to keep my hand from reaching for hers.

"I'm sorry I couldn't tell you I was working undercover," I said after a few moments.

"You were just doing your job."

"Not very well," I replied.

"You caught the Doc and killed Monato. I'd say you did more than very well."

I smiled. "Monato's not dead."

"He's not?" She sounded surprised.

"No. Though I wouldn't mind too much if he was," I admitted. "And I'm sure not unhappy Billy clocked him. But he's not dead, he's just in custody, and he *will* be convicted for Colin's murder...Among other things."

"Good."

I released a breath. "And I'm sorry I didn't tell you about what the tattoo meant."

She didn't answer, and I my heart dropped.

"I think Colin was on to the Doc," I said. "Or at least suspected Monato wasn't working alone. He had a bunch of police files hidden in his bedroom at the house. I found them after I…"

"After you kicked me out," Cass filled in.

"I'm so sorry."

"One of the files was my sister's?" Cass asked.

I nodded and went on. "I swear that was the first time I realized she was connected."

Cass's face filled with pain. "Tell me how it happened."

"Monato and the Doc have been manipulating these girls. They offer them a lot of money, and tell them they're not going to have to *do* anything big. They like them young, and innocent, and desperate. They find them working at the clubs, or waitressing at cheap restaurants. It's like they've got a sixth sense for vulnerability," I explained.

"Like Jeannette. She would've wanted the money for us," Cass agreed sadly.

"And once they've been on a few dates, they offer the girls something simple. An upper to help them stay up late. Then something more to help them sleep. It becomes a cycle, and pretty soon the girls are hooked on drugs. And suddenly the dates are more than dates and they need something to dull their memories of the experience."

"You know a lot about it," Cass said.

"The Doc confessed everything," I told her.

"And Colin?" she wanted to know.

"He was just meant to be infiltrating Monato's business. I know he started to. But I think he suspected Monato was using drugs to hook the girls, then using their addiction to keep them under his thumb. And when he realized some of the girls were ODing...and no one was being held accountable..."

"He had to do something more," Cass filled in.

I nodded. "Exactly."

"Can I ask you something, John?"

"Anything."

"Was any of it real?"

Chapter Thirty-Nine

My heart seized as I asked the question.

It had taken all of three seconds for me to realize I'd made a mistake in running away from him in the police station.

I should have stayed and let John finish.

Only minutes had passed since he'd told me about Jeannette and the tattoo, but I felt like so much more time had gone by.

The last few months of her life suddenly made sense. I thought back to the first moment when I'd *really* noticed the change in my sister.

She'd come into the house on Sunday afternoon—it was the third weekend in a row she'd been away—reeking of cigarette smoke.

"Ew, Jeanie! You smell terrible," I told her.

"You're not even supposed to be home," she snapped.

I was so stunned by her tone that I'd dropped the TV remote. It landed on the floor, splitting open, and the batteries had rolled across the room to where my sister was digging through the coat closet. Jeannette was never short-tempered, even after a twelve hour work day.

"What're you doing?" I asked.

"Looking for money," she muttered.

"What?"

"Looking for money!" she yelled.

I watched her dig around some more, feeling confused. "I thought things at the restaurant had picked up."

She'd been bringing home way more tips than usual. In fact, I'd seen her pay our rent, all in cash, just the week before.

"Jeannette?"

She had stopped looking through the closet, and was staring across the room.

"Hey!"

She jumped a little, then focused a smile in my direction.

"I just ran out, okay?" she said. "And I need to pick something up at the grocery store, and the debit is down at the store."

I frowned, wondering why she sounded like she was parodying her usual cheerful self.

"All right," I agreed. "There's a couple of twenties in my wallet. Just pay me back soon."

She'd given me a hug, taken the money, and left. Somewhere inside, I'd known she wasn't using the money at the grocery store. My sister had deteriorated rapidly after that. I'd never seen the money again, and for some reason, the lie she'd told me that day was representative of every way she'd failed me after.

I felt the same betrayal now. I looked down at my feet, and waited for John's answer. His hand came up, and I braced myself for the feel of his fingers on my chin.

It didn't come.

I brought my eyes up, and met his hurt gaze. His arm was still suspended in the air, and his palm was turned toward my face. I had to force myself to stop from leaning into it.

"As much of it was true as I could manage, Cass," John told me.

"I don't know what that means."

"The club is mine. The Empress Hotel, and a few others like it, are mine."

His face was troubled, and when he didn't meet my gaze, it seemed like he was skirting the issue on purpose. I followed his lead and started walking again. John rushed to catch up.

"Billy?" I asked after a few moments.

"An informant. Colin's to start out with. His daughter got involved with Monato the same way that…" He trailed off.

"The same way that Jeannette did," I filled in.

John cleared his throat. "Yes. Billy wanted to help bring him down."

He paused in front of a four story apartment building, and I stopped and looked at him.

"Monato and Ramirez targeted my sister because she was vulnerable?" I asked.

"Guys like that are experts at picking them out and experts at reeling them in," he replied apologetically.

"And they came after me because I'm that way, too," I stated. "Weak."

"No," John said emphatically. "You're strong. Self-sufficient. I promise you, you're the exact opposite of the kind of girl they target. I think they simply came after you because you look so much like Jeannette. Maybe they thought you knew, like Colin did. Or maybe they didn't even do it consciously. I'm sorry, Cass."

"It's not your fault," I told him

John took a quick step toward me, and I my breath caught in my throat as he bent down to look me in the eyes. I had to work to move my gaze away. And I was immediately regretful when I did. He was so close to me that he took up my whole vision.

The rain had plastered his shirt against his skin, and I could make out the attractive lines of his tattoos through the fabric. I itched to touch them. I tried to back away, and bumped into the wrought iron fence behind me.

I held out my hand. In the dark, the ruby was a dangerously red shield, protecting me from him and tying me to him at the same time.

"Why did you give me this?" I demanded.

"I wanted you to have it," he told me seriously.

"Why?" I could hear the pleading tone, and but I didn't care.

"I saw you outside the tattoo parlour," he admitted. "You and Blair. I noticed you right away."

"Most people notice Blair."

A smile curled his lips, and I stared at them as they moved invitingly with his reply. "I didn't."

"No?"

"Then when I watched you dance in my club…" John trailed off with an appreciative look in his eyes.

"I'm a terrible dancer."

"You're not so bad."

The air around us had shifted somehow, and I the corners of my mouth turned up.

"Liar," I said.

He smiled back at me. "And when I got to haul you around unconscious, that just about cinched it."

I frowned.

"Too soon for jokes?" he murmured.

He'd stepped closer again. He was near enough that I could feel the heat emanating from his chest. I shivered involuntarily.

"Are you cold?" he wanted to know.

I shivered again. "No."

"This is my place." John inclined his head toward the apartment building and replied with a question in his voice.

"Blair told me not to go in with you," I reminded him.

"All right," he agreed. "We won't go in."

He put one hand on my waist and the other on the back of my neck, and pressed his body against me. The fence dug into my back, and I didn't care.

"You want to go in now?" John whispered.

I could barely make myself nod.

Then his lips took mine, quickly, urgently, like he had something to prove. He explored my mouth only briefly, then he moved on to my cheeks and chin and neck.

John's fingers wove through my hair and held onto it tightly, forcing my head back. His tongue found a sensitive spot between my throat and collarbone and then he moved on again. His hands scraped across my skin, and the rain made his palms slick. His aggression left me gasping.

"Inside," I breathed. "Now."

I barely let him get the key through the door before I tossed his shirt to the floor and pulled off my own top. I wrapped my arms around his well-muscled waist and started to slide his pants down.

"Cass," he said hesitantly.

"John," I whispered back.

His lips were against mine, and when I tried to breathe his name a second time, his mouth responded automatically, enveloping my words.

"Bedroom," I murmured when he finally allowed me come up for air.

"Cass," he said again, and tried to pull further away.

I dragged him closer, wondering why he was resisting.

"No one knows me like this," he told me.

"Like what?"

"About Colin. About what my tattoos mean. About anything."

I loosened my grip on him slightly and he went on.

"Don't be sad," he pleaded. "I don't want Blair to be right. I don't want to be the biggest mistake of your life."

I smiled. "John, you're wrong."

"I just don't want you to think I'm the kind of guy who—"

I cut him off by running my thumb along his lips and jaw and then down across his chest. He held very still, as if he didn't trust himself to move. I stood on my tiptoes and with my palms cradling his face, I kissed him gently.

"Blair didn't say being with you was the biggest mistake of my life. She said running away from you was."

"She did?" He sounded genuinely surprised.

"And I already know what kind of man you are," I told him.

He sighed. "Good."

"Bedroom," I said, this time more firmly.

I let him guide me there, and straight into the bed, with no regrets.

255

Chapter Forty

I looked at Cass's sleeping form, silent except for the occasional deep breath.

Her hair was still damp and more than a little matted. Her face was pale, and I noticed a small bruise under her chin. Her arms were scraped and battered, and the foot that stuck out from underneath my sheets was filthy. The rope marks from the trauma two days earlier were highly visible in the beginnings of the dawn light.

But she was beautiful. It overwhelmed me.

As she'd let me lay her down on my scarcely used bed, part of me had wanted to stop her. To ask her if she was really sure, to remind her of the emotionally harrowing occurrences she'd just been through, to ask her if it was too soon. But most of me felt like the weekend had given us a lifetime's worth of experience packed into a few days. And all of me had wanted her.

The sun was starting to make its way up over the horizon, and a few tiny streams of light made their way through my barely open blinds.

"How long you been staring at her like that?"

The sound of Billy's voice startled me, and when I rolled over in surprise, I landed with a thump on my bedroom floor. I scrambled to my feet and hurried to cover Cass more fully with the sheet. I glanced down at myself, clad only in boxer shorts and shrugged. After all, *he* was in *my* house.

"What're you doing here?" I growled, but my heart wasn't in it, and I wound up grinning instead. "I wasn't expecting company."

"I knocked. But you didn't answer."

"I was a bit busy," I told him dryly.

"So things went well?" Billy asked.

"They *were* going well," I corrected with a raised eyebrow.

"Relax," the older man said. "I just wanted to give you this. My last piece of business to deal with before I go back to being a two-bit criminal and you go back to being a cop."

He handed me a flat envelope, and I opened it slowly.

"What is it?" I asked.

But I already knew. Mine and Cass's names were as clear as day under the official, embossed seal.

"Looks like Leo was a little more official—and efficient—than I would've thought," Billy replied.

My heart hammered. "What should I do with it?"

Billy shrugged. "Whatever you want, I guess. Burn it. Frame it. But maybe ask *her* first."

I glanced down at Cass. She was still breathing slowly and evenly. She'd worked an arm free, and I could see the small tattoo on her shoulder.

"Will you keep it?" I'd asked her last night as I'd kissed the fresh ink carefully.

"Of course," she told me. "It means even more now than it did before."

"Maybe you'll get more," I teased.

"Maybe I will," she replied.

I'd closed my eyes and she'd worked her fingers

over the art that covered my chest.

I looked back up to Billy, but he was already gone. I sighed. I was going to have to collect all of my keys from the man sooner rather than later.

"I'm sure there's an out."

Cass was looking at me without a trace of sleepiness in her eyes.

"You're too good at being quiet," I told her.

"I've had lots of practice," she said seriously, then added, "We can probably get a divorce."

"And sully my perfect reputation?" I joked.

She smiled. "An annulment isn't so bad. And easier on the reputation. I speak from experience."

I took her hand.

"Cass," I said. "I don't want an annulment."

"Me neither," she replied softly. "But I do need to tell you something before I start moving my stuff into your house."

I shoved down my immediate panic at her worried tone.

"What's that?" I asked.

"I may have given Blair your Ultralow."

"What?"

"Your bike…"

"I know what it is," I said. "I just don't understand why—"

She cut me off with a thorough kiss.

"All right," I sighed when she let me go. "Blair can keep the bike. But I get to keep you."

"Fair trade," Cass agreed.

A word about the author...

I am a lover of happy endings and big bowls of pasta. I married an Italian man in hopes of getting both. I'm passionate about writing and reading, and a hater of all things housework. I have three beautiful little girls who often interrupt all three of those things. Needless to say, my life is full of unfinished stories and unfinished laundry. When I write, I try to include just enough realism to make my readers say, "Hey, this could be me!" and just enough of the fantastic so that they can add, "Hey, I wish this WAS me!"

Find me on social media (a lot!):
www.facebook.com/MelindaDiLorenzo
on Twitter @melindawrites
www.melindadilorenzowrites.blogspot.com

Thank you for purchasing
this publication of The Wild Rose Press, Inc.
For other wonderful stories of romance,
please visit our on-line bookstore at
www.thewildrosepress.com.

For questions or more information
contact us at
info@thewildrosepress.com.

The Wild Rose Press, Inc.
www.thewildrosepress.com

To visit with authors of
The Wild Rose Press, Inc.
join our yahoo loop at
http://groups.yahoo.com/group/thewildrosepress/

Made in the USA
San Bernardino, CA
27 October 2014